Cold Karma

By

Eldred Bird

Other books by Eldred Bird:

Killing Karma

Catching Karma

author@eldredbird.com

Contents

Dedication

This book is dedicated to all Cold Case Detectives everywhere. These remarkable men and women spend countless hours sifting through mountains of materials and evidence looking for the one needle in an old haystack that will bring justice and closure for victims and their families.

Chapter 1

James McCarthy strolled through the Courthouse Square Park, hands in his pockets and the crisp October air filling his lungs. While Phoenix and the rest of the valley sweltered in the early afternoon heat, Prescott was a welcome change. The higher elevation and nearly unbroken canopy of trees covering the park made all the difference. Autumn arrived in the mountain community much earlier than at his home in the city.

The walk from his car to the little Mexican restaurant off the square was just what James needed after spending the morning being grilled by Detective David Alexander. The Senior Crime Scene Investigator from the Yavapai County Sheriff's Office went over every detail of the statement James had given about the shooting a couple of months earlier. Alexander pounded him with questions, barely giving him time to answer one before hitting him with another.

James was sure the detective was trying to trip him up — to find a hole in his story — but he never stumbled. Every detail in his written statement was accurate right down to the punctuation. Detective Alexander was a perfectionist, but James was more so. It was his business. The freelance writer had built his reputation on accurate observation and concise delivery of information. To be more precise, he had built Josh McDaniel's reputation on it.

To the handful of people in the know Josh McDaniel was the name James used when he wrote, but to James he was much more. Josh was the mask he hid behind. Fearing his youth and inexperience would hurt his credibility, James created the persona early in his career. He built such a distinctive personality around the character that Josh now occupied a permanent space in James' brain—not so much a second personality, but more of a separate entity. The two conversed whenever James faced a challenge. More often than not, they argued.

When forced to make public appearances, James would bite the bullet and dress as his alter ego. Not at all happy with the task, he considered it a necessary evil. A visit to Dugan's Public House was usually required to get in the proper frame of mind. A stiff drink at his family's bar relaxed James just enough to allow Josh to come out and play. But today was not about Josh.

James stepped off the curb and jogged across the street seconds before the traffic light changed, releasing a wave of cars and a cloud of blue-gray exhaust. He walked around the corner, pulled the door to the restaurant open and smiled.

The welcoming aroma of chilis, spices and fresh tortillas filled the small dining room. No more than a dozen tables were crowded into the brightly painted establishment. From a seat in the far corner, a stocky Native American man in a tan uniform waved him over. As James approached, the man stood and extended his hand.

"Deputy Yazzi," James said shaking his hand. "Thanks for meeting me."

"Always happy to see you, Stray Dog." Yazzi motioned to the waitress as they took their seats.

Deputy Nestor Yazzi had a habit of giving people nicknames. Stray Dog was the name he'd pinned on James when they first met in the foothills of the Bradshaw Mountains. The young writer had been helping his brother, Will Dugan, a Phoenix PD narcotics detective, investigate a homicide. Upon learning James was not a blood relative, but unofficially adopted into the Dugan clan, "Stray Dog" were the first words to pass Nestor's thin lips. The label stuck.

Nestor spoke in his usual slow cadence and emotionless tone. "I told you before, you can drop the deputy and just call me Nestor. There's no need for titles between friends."

"Sorry, I was raised to respect my eld—" James cut himself off. He picked up a menu and propped it up in front of his reddening face. "So, what's good here?"

"Everything." A small grin cracked Nestor's stone face as the waitress approached their table. "Don't worry, Stray Dog. Elder is a term of respect with my people."

After they placed their orders, Nestor settled back in his chair — James did not. His back remained rigid as he unwrapped the napkin around his silverware. He fidgeted with the paper band that held the bundle together, shredding it into confetti sized pieces.

"You need another one?" Nestor pulled the paper strip off his napkin and held it out. "Alexander must have been pretty rough on you."

"I don't think he likes me." James set the mangled paper to the side and folded his hands on the table. "He must have asked me the same questions at least twenty times."

"Did you give him the same answers?"

James nodded. "Down to the letter."

"Then there's nothing to worry about." Nestor folded his paper up and dropped it on the table. "I read your statement. I didn't see anything that wasn't supported by the evidence."

"It felt like he was trying to make me nervous . . . like he wanted me to mess up so he could accuse me of something."

"Alexander is wrapped a little tight," Nestor replied as the waitress set their drinks on the table. "You contributed a lot to solving those murders. Your name came up quite a bit in your brother's reports."

"I shouldn't have been so involved, but Will—"

Nestor raised a hand to stop him. "Don't apologize. Your insights were valuable and your instincts were good. Alexander doesn't like it when civilians get involved in a case. He was probably trying to scare you off—keep you away until the rest of the investigation is finished."

"All he had to do was ask. I already told Will I'm not playing cop anymore."

"Too bad, you're good at it." Nestor crossed his arms. "So, if it's not about the case, why did you offer to buy me lunch today?"

James took a sip of his iced tea and cleared his throat. "I need your help with something."

Nestor raised an eyebrow. "You in some kind of trouble?"

"It's nothing like that," James replied. "I need some advice. You talked me through a pretty tough time the day you saved my life. Do you remember?"

"Every detail." Nestor gave a small nod. "You went out alone and got in over your head."

11

James nodded sheepishly. "You told me something that day. You said I wasn't ready to be on my own yet—that I still needed a guide on my path."

"I remember. I said you have great knowledge, but experience teaches you things books can't."

"Exactly." James took a deep breath and looked Nestor in the eyes. "You have a lot of experience . . . and wisdom, too. I was hoping you might be willing to share some of it with me—to be my guide."

Nestor smiled. "I'm flattered you would ask. How can I help?"

"My brother, Donny, and his wife asked me to be Godfather to their baby when it arrives."

"Congratulations, that's quite an honor." Nestor reached across the table and shook James' hand. "So, what's the problem?"

"As Godfather, I'm supposed to give the child moral and spiritual guidance."

"You're an intelligent, upstanding man. Any child would be lucky to have you look after their soul." Nestor shrugged. "I don't see what your concern is."

"Well . . ." James hesitated and took another drink. "It's just that . . . Donny and Jen are Catholic, and I'm not," he finally blurted out.

Nestor uncrossed his arms and leaned forward. "Do you believe in God?"

"That's the problem." James slumped and let out a sigh. "I don't know what I believe."

"Now I see your dilemma." Nestor relaxed back into his chair. "How do you teach a child what you don't know yourself?"

James opened his mouth to speak, but closed it when the waitress stopped at the table to deliver their lunches. As soon as she moved on to the next table, he tried again.

"My mother raised me with a strict moral code, but she never talked about God. She seemed to think that if you put positive energy out into the universe, positive energy would come back to you—same thing for negative."

"You get what you give—good or bad," Nestor interjected. "Karma."

James nodded. "That's one word for it. When my father died, I think she felt she'd done something wrong and was being punished for it. She didn't want anything bad to happen to me, so she spent the rest of her life making sure the balance was always in my favor."

"A bit misguided," Nestor replied. "But I can understand her reasoning."

James continued. "Well, as a result I grew up sheltered—closed off from the world. I had no idea what I was missing until my mother passed, and then I met the Dugans. When they took me into their family, my life changed . . . for the better."

"And now you don't want to disappoint them?"

"Exactly." James pushed the food around on his plate, and then set his fork down without taking a bite. "They're trusting me with this huge responsibility, and I don't want to let them down."

Nestor closed his eyes and thought for a moment. James sat motionless watching the deputy's head slowly bob up and down. Finally, Nestor opened his eyes, and spoke.

"I can't tell you what to believe, Stray Dog, but I'd be honored to help you search for your own answers."

James breathed a sigh of relief. "Thank you. You have no idea what this means to me. I don't know how I'll ever repay you."

"How about we make a trade?" Nestor asked with a smile. "I'll guide you on your journey, if you'll help me solve a difficult case."

Chapter 2

Detective William Dugan walked down the hallway of the Yavapai County Medical Examiner's Office, one hand in the pocket of his new, black jeans, the other clutching a leather portfolio. His blue polo shirt was neatly tucked in and his shoes sported a near perfect shine. His hair, trimmed and combed, framed his clean shaven face. Even his bushy eyebrows had been tamed. This clean-cut image was not one the tall, muscular cop normally presented.

On most days, greasy reddish-brown hair hung down to his shoulders and he sported a scruffy beard. The colors of his grungy clothes often clashed, and they generally reeked of sweat and body odor. It wasn't a lifestyle choice, but a requirement of Will's job. The Phoenix PD narcotics officer spent a good percentage of his time undercover, posing as a drug dealer named Willy-D. Today, that was not the image he wished to project.

Will stopped at the end of the hall and stared at the slate-blue door in front of him. Small beads of sweat formed on the brow and upper lip of the normally confident cop. The reason for cleaning up his image sat in the next room, unaware of his approach. Will raised one arm and then the other, giving each armpit a quick sniff. With a nod of self-approval, he straightened his back and opened the heavy steel door.

Dr. Sarah O'Donnell looked up from her desk. The Deputy Medical Examiner pushed her tortoise shell glasses up with one finger and tucked her long, red hair behind her ear. When Will locked onto her emerald green eyes, he froze in place, unable to speak.

"May I help you?"

"Um . . . I'm um . . ." He took a deep breath and tried to regain his composure. "I'm Will Dugan . . . from Phoenix. We met in Mike Miller's office, remember?"

"Detective Dugan?" The young doctor's eyes lit up. "I didn't recognize you. You look . . . different."

"I guess I looked a little rough the first time you saw me." Will glanced down and smoothed the front of his shirt. "I was doing some undercover work — you know, related to the Green Legion homicides."

"Yes, I remember reading your reports." She motioned toward a chair in front of her desk. "What brings you in today?"

Will took a seat and fumbled with his portfolio. "My brother had to go in for another interview with Detective Alexander, so I hitched a ride up to Prescott with him. I figured I'd take the opportunity to tie up some loose ends — maybe see how you're doing with identifying the rest of the bodies."

"I'm still waiting for the DNA results on several samples, but you didn't have to come all the way up here for that. You could've just emailed me." Sarah took her glasses off and laid them to the side. "I thought your part of the investigation was done."

"It is, but I figured with the murders being drug related and all, maybe some of the victims could be tied to a few of my open cases."

"Sergeant Miller already has the reports on the victims we've identified. I'm pretty sure you were copied on them as well." Sarah crossed her arms on the desk and leaned forward. "Why are you really here?"

"Like I said, Jimmy was coming up anyway and I figured it might be nice to get out of town for the day." Will squirmed in his seat. "But as long as I *am* here, um . . . Jimmy's meeting Yazzi for lunch, so I'm kind of on my own and I don't really know what's around here."

"Detective Dugan." Sarah sat up straight and smiled. "Are you asking me out?"

"For lunch," Will stammered. "Just a couple of colleagues having lunch."

"Detective—"

"Call me Will," he interjected. "Everybody just calls me Will."

"Not everybody." Sarah raised an eyebrow and smiled. "I heard Nestor calls you Packrat."

Will deflated like a punctured tire and sunk back in his chair. "For somebody who doesn't talk much, that guy's got a big mouth. I think he hates me."

"He doesn't hate you," Sarah reassured. "If he didn't like you, he wouldn't bother to give you a nickname."

"Really?" Will shook his head. "So why does he give me so much crap?"

"That's just his way of teaching you. I'll admit he's an acquired taste, but give him a chance. He'll grow on you."

"Yeah, like a foot fungus," Will scoffed. "You seem to know him pretty well. Has he given you a name yet?"

"Yes. He calls me something in Navajo I can't pronounce." The corners of Sarah's mouth curled up. "His wife told me it means red squirrel."

Will's face scrunched up. "I can buy the red part because of your hair, but a squirrel? I don't get it. You don't come off as squirrely to me."

Sarah let out a laugh, followed by a small

snort. "I don't think that's what he means. Like a squirrel, I tend to stock up on things for use in the future—office supplies are a perfect example. They're kind of my weakness."

She swiveled her chair around and opened the tall cabinet behind her. Neat stacks of legal pads, staples, boxes of envelopes, and other items filled the shelves. Sarah turned back and slid the top drawer of her desk open, revealing perfectly arranged rows of pens, pencils, and markers.

Will sat back up and peered over the desk, his eyes wide. "Holy crap. That's not a weakness, that's a full on addiction!"

"Working in narcotics, I guess you'd know."

"Oh yeah, I've seen this before." Will smiled and nodded. "You haven't met my brother Jimmy yet. His desk drawer looks just like that. His girlfriend swapped a couple of markers around once just to screw with him. I swear he felt some kind of cosmic disturbance."

"I think I got it from my father." Sarah lowered her voice and mugged a gruff expression. "'A place for everything, and everything in its place.' That's his favorite saying."

"My partner Carl says I tend to lean more toward a place for everything, and everything *out* of place. Kinda drives him up the wall."

19

Sarah shuddered. "I can feel his pain. I'm sure if I saw your desk, I'd be compelled to clean and organize it."

Will grinned. "You have an open invitation anytime you're in Phoenix."

Sarah pushed the drawer back in and closed the cabinet. "Speaking of invitations—now that we've shared our dirty little secrets, do you still want to buy me lunch?"

"Absolutely," Will stood and pointed over his shoulder with an extended thumb. "I think I saw a barbeque joint next to an office supply store on the way into town."

Chapter 3

James and Nestor strolled down the sidewalk opposite the Courthouse Square Park and stopped at the signal in front of the historic Hotel St. Michael.

"You have time to come by and take a quick look at the case today?" Nestor asked.

James checked his watch. "Sure. Will has my car and he's not going to be back for a while. Can I get a ride back to the station with you?"

"No need," Nestor replied. "I have copies of everything at my house. It's just a couple blocks from here."

"I could use the walk after that lunch." James grimaced and rubbed his stomach as they crossed the street and turned down the hill. "Do you keep copies of all of your active cases at home?"

"No, just this one." Nestor kept his eyes straight ahead. "And technically, it's not my case."

"Whose case is it?"

"Nobody's," he answered without breaking pace. "It's a cold case — been on the shelf for years."

James scratched his head. "Then why do you have copies of the files at your house?"

"Because I plan on solving it." Nestor glanced sideways and winked. "Or maybe you will, Stray Dog."

James stretched his steps to keep up with Yazzi. "This isn't just about getting a case off the books, right? If you're motivated enough to have copies at home, I'd almost bet this case is personal."

The deputy didn't speak, and only gave a single nod. They spent the rest of the walk in silence. At the bottom of the hill, Nestor turned and headed a few houses up the street before stopping. He opened the gate in the low chain link fence and waved James toward the front porch. As they stepped through the gate a loud bark burst through the screen door, followed by a bounding mass of white fur, teeth and tongue. James froze in place as the massive canine closed in on him.

"CHINDI!" A short, round woman called sharply as she reached out and grabbed the dog by the collar. "*Chindi! Huc-quo!*"

Nestor grinned and patted James on the shoulder as he stepped around him. "It's okay. He won't bite, but he might knock you over."

When the woman released the dog, he ran straight to Nestor, jumping and licking between excited barks. After giving the animal a few good scratches in just the right place, Nestor snapped his fingers and pointed at the house. The dog ran back up on the porch and sat next to the woman.

"His name is Chindi," Nestor said as he beckoned for James to follow. "It means devil."

"Devil?" James kept his feet planted firmly on the gravel path. "Are you sure he won't bite me?"

"Never been around dogs, huh?" The woman let the dog back in the house and closed the door. "He's like Nestor — all bark."

"My brother Donny has a dog, a Jack Russell," James replied, his voice shaking. "But he only weighs about twelve pounds."

"Terriers," the woman scoffed. "Attitudes are bigger than their bodies."

"My wife, Mona." Nestor pushed James up to the steps.

He extended his hand. "James McCarthy."

"Stray Dog," she replied, grabbing his hand and pulling him up on the porch. "You're too skinny. Both of you, inside. I'll make lunch."

"Um . . . thanks, but we already ate," James said with a sheepish smile.

Mona Yazzi glared at Nestor, lowered her chin, and furrowed her brow. "Did you go to that Mexican place again? You know what the doctor said." She shook her fist. "You give yourself a heart attack and I'll beat you to death!"

"You'll try," Nestor replied, smiling and giving her a peck on the cheek as he passed. "Come on, Stray Dog, I'll show you the case files."

James followed Nestor into the house and down the narrow hallway to a small office. He kept an eye over his shoulder and locked onto the panting beast inches off his heels. Nestor grabbed a folding chair out of the closet and set it up next to the desk. Once Chindi curled up on a pillow in the corner, James breathed a sigh of relief and sat down. Nestor slid a well worn file box out from under the desk and pulled off the lid.

"This is everything I've got." He pulled out several folders and placed them on the desk. "Been through all of it a hundred times."

"What makes you think I'm going to be able to help? I mean, you're a trained detective. I'm just a writer."

"You're a smart man." Nestor pushed the folders toward him. "And maybe new eyes will see something different."

James opened the thickest folder and scanned several pages. "A missing person case?" He looked at few more pages. "Who's Virgil Deschene?"

"My best friend since grade school."

"So this *is* personal."

Nestor picked up a framed photograph off the desk and handed it James. "We played football together in high school—Virgil's on the bottom row, third from the left."

"Is that you next to him?" James squinted and held the picture closer. "You look like twins."

"They called us Double-Trouble." Nestor smiled as James handed the picture back. "We could break any offensive line you put in front of us. Virgil still holds the school record for the most sacks in one season."

James thumbed through the file. "According to this, it's been fourteen years since he disappeared. Do you have any idea where he might have gone?"

"I don't think he went anywhere." Nestor's smile faded. "My gut tells me he's dead."

"What makes you say that?" James asked. "Was there evidence of a fight? Blood or anything?"

"Nothing at the last place he was supposed to be." Nestor handed him another folder. "Here's the CSI report. He was out working a mining claim like he did just about every weekend. When he didn't show up for work Monday morning, his daughter drove out to look for him. He was gone and so was his gear."

"If his gear wasn't there, how do you know he was?" James asked. "Maybe he never made it out there in the first place."

"He had a partner—Emery Lewis. He said

Virgil was fine when he left him Saturday morning."

James opened the file folder and read the first page.

"Uh-oh . . ." He took a deep breath, held up a report and pointed at the name on the coversheet. "Please tell me there's another David Alexander."

"Nope." Nestor shook his head. "Same man you spent the morning with."

"He already hates me." James dropped the file on the desk and pushed it away like he expected the pages to burst into flames at any moment. "I don't think I should be messing around in one of his cases."

"It's not his case," Nestor pushed the folder back toward James. "He just investigated the area where Virgil was camped. It was one of his first assignments after being promoted."

"Talking about that Alexander fellow?" Mona walked in and set a tray with two glasses of ice and a pitcher of tea on the desk. "Man's a jackass—has a dark spirit." She turned and walked back out of the room without waiting for a response.

"He's going to blow up." James opened the folder again and stared at the coversheet. "You said it yourself—he doesn't like private citizens getting involved in police business."

Nestor shrugged as the corners of his mouth turned up slightly. "He can't say anything if you work for the County Sherriff's Office."

James' eyes widened. "You want me to become a police officer?"

"Special Investigator," Nestor replied with a grin. "I have money in my budget for a consultant. I can bring in anyone I want to help me, and he has no say in the matter."

"Won't that just make him more angry?"

"Maybe." Nestor smiled, poured a glass of tea, and leaned back in his chair. "That's just a bonus."

Chapter 4

Missy Franklin stepped through the door of James' house in the historic district of downtown Phoenix and tossed her purse onto the couch. Her long dark ponytail flipped through the air as she turned to find her boyfriend sitting at the dining room table hunched over pile of file folders. Missy walked up behind him and laid a hand on his shoulder.

"What are you working on, Jimmy?"

"WHAT THE—" James lept out of his chair like he'd been hit with a cattle prod, and spun around clutching his chest. "Oh my God, you almost gave me a heart attack. I didn't hear you come in."

"Sorry about that." She laughed, hugged him, and gave him a quick kiss. "You were pretty into this stuff. What is it?"

"It's a cold case. I'm helping Nestor with it."

Missy smirked. "So, you guys are on a first name basis now, huh?"

"He said that's what I should call him since we're friends," James replied. "But he still calls me Stray Dog."

"I love that name. I think it's cute." She eyed the piles of paper covering the table. "I guess this means he agreed to help you with your problem."

"He suggested we make a trade. If I help

28

him with this case, he'll help me figure out what I believe."

"Sounds fair." Missy picked up one of the folders and pulled out a stack of photos. "Is this the crime scene?"

"That's the first question I need to answer." James sat back down and shuffled a few pages. "It's a missing person case. If the man left on his own then there *is* no crime scene, because there was no crime."

"What kind of stuff are you looking for?" Missy studied one of the pictures. "I don't see anything but dirt, trees, and bushes."

"There's a tractor and some hand tools in a few of the other images, but nothing unusual." James looked at the pile of photos and shook his head. "I can't put my finger on it, but something about these pictures bothers me . . . like I'm missing some detail."

"If anybody can find a missing detail, it's you. You're the king of over-analyzing. What was the guy doing when he disappeared?"

"He was working a mining claim near the Verde River west of Perkinsville."

"The place where the train from Clarkdale stops?"

"Yes, the Verde Canyon Railroad. The claim was upstream from there." James pulled a map out from under the pile of papers and pointed to a plot bordered in red ink. "He was camping out for the weekend and doing some prospecting."

Missy read the name on the map. "Hell Canyon? Doesn't exactly sound like the kind of place I'd want to spend the night."

"According to his partner, he spent a lot of nights out there by himself—at least two or three times a month," James replied. "His daughter said the same thing when they interviewed her."

"So Yazzi wants you to help him find this guy?"

"Or figure out who killed him." James looked directly in her blue eyes. "Nestor thinks he's dead."

"Oh . . ." Missy pulled out a chair and sat down. "How long has he been gone?"

"Fourteen years."

"That's a long time," she sighed. "It's not like you can just go search the place again to find more evidence. There wouldn't be anything left."

"No," James shook his head. "I'm kind of limited to what's on this table, but I can't seem to get a complete picture in my head."

"Then let's build the picture." Missy started picking all of the photos out of the pile and began shuffling through them. "How do you feel about jigsaw puzzles?"

"You're brilliant!" James jumped up, grabbed Missy by the shoulders, and kissed her on both cheeks. "If we look for details in the images that overlap, maybe we can piece together the whole scene."

James cleared one end of the table and they both started laying out photos. They shifted and turned the images around, lining things up whenever they found a match. Over the next hour the scene began to take shape, though not without issues.

"I see a lot of gaps, and some of this stuff just doesn't fit," Missy complained. "They're all different sizes and different angles. Whoever took these was moving around an awful lot."

"The investigator was probably trying to get specific details," James replied. "I don't think he was expecting anyone to build the images into one big panorama, but this should still give me a better idea of where things are in relation to each other."

"This is it." Missy slid the last photo into place and stepped back to take it all in. "Kind of a mess, but I guess it'll have to do."

"Maybe this will help to clear things up." James turned his laptop around. "Here's the satellite map of the area. If we can match up the landmarks in the background to the ones on the map, it should tell us which direction we're looking in each image."

"Okay, I see the San Francisco Peaks in this one." Missy pointed to a photo in the middle of group. "They should be somewhere to the northeast, right?"

"Almost exactly 45 degrees northeast," James replied. "The claim is on the south bank of the Verde, so the next group to the left must be looking north toward the river."

Missy inspected the grouping. "How come I don't see it? There's a mountain in the background, but I don't see water."

"That must be Bill Williams Mountain." James scrolled the map around on the screen. "There it is. The river is down in the canyon—that means this group of pictures were all taken up on the mesa."

Missy nodded. "That explains why I don't see a mine in any of the pictures. Your guy must have worked down in the canyon and stored his equipment on the flats above."

"That sounds right." James smiled. "You're pretty good at this."

"I'm learning," she replied, pointing at the satellite image again. "This road coming from the south looks like the only way in. It should be in those pictures over there."

James moved to the next photo grouping. "Got it. I see the police vehicles parked down the road."

Missy stepped back and crossed her arms. "I guess we know where all of this stuff is now, but what is it telling us?"

"I don't know." James scratched his head and pondered the tangled mass of images stretching across the table. "Seeing the big picture is a step in the right direction, but something still looks out of place. I just can't put my finger on it."

"Maybe you need to get away from it for a few minutes." She took his hand and led him over to the couch. "Do you know why Yazzi is convinced the guy is dead?"

"He knew Virgil Deschene pretty well," James replied. "They grew up together and went to the same school—even joined the Marines at the same time. Nestor said there's no way he'd take off like that."

"People do weird stuff all the time, Jimmy. Just look at my family." Missy laid her head on his shoulder. "You never know what's going on inside somebody's head"

"According to Nestor, Virgil's daughter was getting married and he was pretty excited about it. After his wife died, she was his whole world. I don't think he would have left her like that."

"You're right," Missy agreed. "If the guy was anything like Yazzi, there's no way he'd ditch his daughter right before her wedding. Maybe somebody killed him for his money. He was looking for gold, right?"

"They hadn't found anything yet," James replied. "And as far as I can tell, he didn't *have* any money. His bank account was just about empty and he didn't make that much anyway."

"What about his partner? Wouldn't he have ended up with the claim all to himself if Virgil disappeared?"

"I've read a couple of interviews detectives did with his partner, Emery Lewis. He never worked the mine after Virgil left. Lewis just packed up the equipment and abandoned the claim." James leaned his head back and closed his eyes. "I can't stop thinking about the pictures. I know I'm missing something, but what?"

"*Dinner!*" Missy jumped up from the couch and pulled James to his feet. "We're missing dinner! We were supposed to be at the pub twenty minutes ago!"

Chapter 5

Missy and James pushed their way through the crowded Irish themed pub and approached the bar. Not a single stool sat vacant. Donny Dugan ran between customers, pouring drinks, mixing cocktails, and grabbing empty glasses. Despite his size, the big man moved with speed and grace. His every motion had purpose—no time or energy wasted. Donny grew up behind the bar at Dugan's Public House and it showed. This was his domain.

"Sorry we're late." James leaned over the end of the bar. "What's going on? I've never see it this crazy in here."

Donny slid a pint glass under a tap and answered in his light Irish accent. "Social media. Some fool posted 'bout a well known writer hangin' out here from time to time, and it went viral—place has been a madhouse ever since."

"Who is it?" James craned his neck and searched the crowd.

Missy put a hand on his shoulder and pulled him back down. "Maybe Josh McDaniel? And I'll bet I know what fool posted it." She raised an eyebrow and gave Donny a stern look.

"I thought it might be good for business if word got out." Donny set several beers in front of an exhausted waitress. She loaded them on her tray and disappeared back into the sea of patrons. "I never expected anything like this . . . and it's mostly women!"

James lowered his head and ducked behind Missy. "These people are all here because of me?"

"No, they're here because of Josh." Donny grinned and stroked his bushy red beard. "And I'd keep your voice down if you don't want to get mobbed."

Missy laughed. "I wouldn't worry about it. It's so loud in here you could stick a knife between somebody's ribs and nobody would hear the scream." She took James' hand and pulled him toward the kitchen door. "Come on. Let's go find your mom before some psycho fan-girl recognizes you."

Missy led the way as they headed through the kitchen and into the storage area. They found Margie Dugan seated in the back office, hunched over a pile of paperwork and banging away at a computer keyboard with two fingers. She raised her head as the pair walked toward her.

"Jimmy!" The little white-haired Irish woman jumped up, wrapped her arms around his chest, and squeezed the air out of him. "I'm glad you made it through that mess unscathed."

"Sorry we're late," he replied once he got his breath back. "We kind of got into something

36

and lost track of time."

"Oh really." She winked at Missy and hugged her as well. "Don't worry about it. Plans have changed a little, Jimmy. I'm afraid your bonehead brother miscalculated a wee bit. Now we're all runnin' willy-nilly tryin' to get a handle on things. Family dinner's gonna have to wait for another day."

"Donny told us what he did. I guess I'll be hiding out in the back until things die down."

Margie smiled and patted his arm. "Long as you don't come in lookin' like Mr. McDaniel for a while, you should be fine."

"You ought to have your next book signing here," Missy quipped. "Looks like you won't have any trouble getting fans to show up."

"Don't you *dare* make that joke in front of Donny! The boy's liable to latch on and run with it." Margie sat back down at the computer. "We already have to order more of just about everything, and the daytime staff hasn't been able to go home yet."

"I've got to hand it to him. He certainly knows how to drum up business." James looked back toward the door. "I just hope the Fire Marshal doesn't show up."

"Oh, he's already been here." Margie smiled and winked. "Donny gave him a double shot of Bushmills and promised to get him an autographed book. He left a happy man."

"He bribed a city official?" Missy shook her head. "I hope Will didn't see that. He'd probably get a kick out of arresting his own brother."

"Speakin' of Willy, he's runnin' a bit late, too," Margie replied. "Said he was bringin' some doctor with him."

James perked up like a hunting dog alerting to a game-bird. "Dr. O'Donnell?"

"Right—O'Donnell. I think he works on the dead bodies."

James bit his lip and fought back a grin. "Um . . . he's a *she*."

"And Will wants to work on *her* body," Missy blurted out.

"Willy's interested in a lady doctor?" Margie rolled her eyes. "I hate to be the one to say it, but he might be aimin' a bit high. The boy's never had more than a couple of dates with the same girl."

"Why do you think that is?" James asked.

"You're so naive." Missy rubbed his back and kissed him on the cheek. "In case you haven't noticed, your brother acts like a jackass around women."

"Maybe it's just a professional relationship. They are working on the same case."

Missy stifled a laugh. "Right, Jimmy, his interest is *purely* professional. Have you seen the way he's been acting? I swear he drools every time her name comes up."

"Like Pavlov's dog?"

"You know, a year ago I wouldn't have had a clue what you're talking about." Missy shook her head. "Now, I can actually picture it."

"I know the feeling." Margie pointed at her computer. "You're the first one to get me to touch this infernal contraption. We all use our brains a little more since you came around, Jimmy."

"Well, all but Will," Missy added.

As if conjured by the mention of his name, Will Dugan stepped through the door and held it open for Dr. O'Donnell.

"What in the hel- . . . heck is going on out there?" Will asked as the door swung closed behind him. "There's not an empty seat in the house."

"Celebrity sighting," Margie winked at James, and then stood up. "You must be the doctor I heard about. Willy, where's your manners? Aren't you going to introduce us?"

"Dr. Sarah O'Donnell, this is my mom, Margie Dugan."

"Nice to meet you, Mrs. Dugan." The doctor extended her hand.

Margie bypassed it and went straight for in for a hug. "Just call me Mum—everyone else does."

"And you can call me Sarah." She returned the squeeze.

"This is Missy Franklin." Will pointed at Missy, then James. "And my brother, Jimmy."

"Of course." Sarah shook his hand. "I hear you're working on a cold case with Deputy Yazzi."

"It's a missing person. A man named Virgil Deschene."

Sarah nodded. "I should have guessed. He had me look at the same case a couple of years ago."

"Why did he come to you?" James asked, cocking his head like a puppy. "No body was ever found, so there was no autopsy."

"That doesn't matter to Nestor. He solicits input from anyone he thinks can help. If he asks, it means he respects you."

Will crossed his arms. "He hasn't asked me yet."

"You two had a rough start. Give it time." Sarah turned back to James. "Have you made any progress?"

"Not yet. I've been reading through everything and trying to get familiar with the details. We laid all of the photos out into one big panorama to get a better understanding of the area."

Missy shot her hand up. "That was my idea!"

Will chuckled. "You had an idea?"

Missy raised a fist, but before she could take a swing, Sarah smacked Will on the arm with the back of her hand. "That wasn't very nice."

"I like her already," Missy giggled.

"Well, it *was* a good idea," Sarah replied. "Sometimes it helps to step back and take a look at the big picture."

"I do have a better feel for the area now," James replied. "But it really hasn't helped as much as I'd hoped. If anything, it's created more questions."

"Like what?" Will asked, rubbing his arm.

James shrugged. "It's not anything specific. It's more of a feeling—like I'm missing some detail."

"It can be frustrating." Sarah gritted her teeth. "I know sometimes I'll stare at the same x-rays for what feels like hours."

Will shook his head. "I agree stepping back works when you're trying to get the big picture, but sometimes you've gotta look at it from the *inside* to really know what's going on. You know, put yourself in the picture."

"Like when you go undercover?" James asked.

"Exactly. You can't get the real nitty-gritty until you're in the middle of it. Maybe you should go out there and take a look around." Will shook a finger at James. "Just don't go out alone this time."

"I learned my lesson." James sighed and leaned against the wall. "Besides, it wouldn't look anywhere near the same now. It's been fourteen years."

"Yeah, even the plants would be different." Missy took his hand and rubbed it. "Too bad you don't have a time machine."

James thought for a moment, and then straightened up. The corners of his mouth rose.

"I may not have a time machine, but that *does* give me an idea!"

Chapter 6

As he sat in front of his computer, James could swear he heard Josh McDaniel chuckle inside his brain.

You know you look like a total goof in that contraption, right?

"Laugh all you want. It looks like it's going to accomplish what I hoped it would." James pulled off his headgear and set it on the desk next to his keyboard.

So you're trying to build a time machine?

"Sort of. I may not be able to physically go back in time, but the display in Virtual Reality hood will get me as close to it as possible." James placed a photo on the bed of his scanner and closed the top. "Once I get the rest of these images loaded into the software and lined up, it'll be like I'm standing in the middle of the crime scene fourteen years ago."

That setup looks like it cost a lot more than Yazzi's paying you.

"It didn't cost me anything. I called the company that created the imaging software and told them what I want to do. When I said Josh McDaniel might write an article about it, they offered to loan me the hardware as well."

So, you dropped my name and they just handed

over a couple grand worth of tech?

"After I explained things, they were really interested in the possible law enforcement applications. I pointed out that virtual recreation of crime scenes could open up a whole new market for their product."

Ah, so you appealed to their wallets. Gutsy move.

"I figured the worst that could happen is they'd say no."

Okay, now you've got me curious. Let's see how this works.

James spent the next few hours scanning photos and importing them into the program. He tweaked, twisted and warped each picture with the help of the software, stitching them together into a single, 360 degree image. After the last photo was inserted, several holes still remained. With the click of a mouse, James directed the program to automatically fill in the open spaces by extrapolating colors and textures, and smoothing them into the gaps. He donned the headgear again to view his handiwork.

"Wow! This is amazing. It's almost like being there."

I don't know . . . I'm a little underwhelmed.

"What do you mean?" James turned his head from side to side, raising and lowering his chin as he went. "It's even tracking my movements. I feel like I'm right in the middle of the scene."

I expected it to have more depth — like the sample images, or one of those 3D superhero movies Missy drags you to. Everything looks flat.

"Those were shot with stereo cameras. The pictures I had to use for this reconstruction were just standard images. They were never intended to be used for something like this, so there's no separation to create the 3D effect."

Ah, the software's feeding the same image to both eyes, instead of a right and left view.

"Exactly, but it'll work for my purposes."

Okay, so you've managed to step back in time. Now what?

"Just a couple of quick settings, and then we'll get a better look at the big picture."

James adjusted the contrast and then turned his head, tilting up and down as he went. The image scrolled and tilted as well, matching his movements. When he saw the twin ruts of a dirt road he stopped, moved the mouse pointer to the center of the image, and right-clicked. A menu popped up in the middle of his field of vision. When he selected one of the options, a line of numbers appeared over the image circling his head.

"According to the map, this road came into Virgil's camp from due south." James grabbed the ring with the mouse pointer and pulled it around until the heading 180 degrees was lined up over the road. "Now I'll know which way I'm oriented while I'm searching."

Searching for what?

"I wish I knew." James tilted his head up and down as he slowly rotated counter-clockwise in his chair. "I guess I'm looking for anything that seems unusual or out of place."

This is someplace you've never been before, and it's fourteen years in the past. How are you going to know what's out of place?

"I'm not sure, but something seemed off when Missy and I were going through the pictures. I'm hoping whatever it was will stand out from this point of view."

Well, all I see so far is a whole lot of nothing.

"Yeah, and that bothers me." James lowered his head and scanned the ground. "Look at all this stuff stacked and organized here— shovels, picks, a toolbox." James turned to the north. "Even a tractor just left sitting there."

That's a backhoe.

"Whatever. If you were going to take off, why would you pack up everything else but leave these things behind?"

Maybe he left in a hurry.

"I don't think so. The whole area is cleaned up. I don't even see tire tracks leading to where the tractor is parked. Why would you take the time to wipe out something like that if you're leaving in a hurry?" James turned a full circle, scanning the area. "I can't even tell where he had his tent, or where he parked his truck."

Turn back to the road for a second. You know what else I see?

James looked back to the south. "All I see are the police vehicles down the road."

Do you see anything else?

"No, just a few footprints — probably from the officers and the person taking the pictures."

Exactly. If Virgil drove out of here, where are his tire tracks? I don't think that rust bucket of his had wings.

"You're right. All I see is one set of tire tracks that stop and turn around before they get all the way up here, but that's it. The police didn't drive up this far, so those tracks must be from his daughter when she came out here to check on him."

It looks like somebody cleaned up the scene. The question is why.

James thought for a moment. "Well, the way I see it there are a couple of possibilities. Virgil may have had some reason to disappear that we don't know about yet, and he took what he thought he might need. He may have cleaned up the area to throw off anyone who might go looking for him."

What's the point of doing that? There's only one way out of here, so he had to go that way.

"True. Wiping out his tracks wouldn't have bought him anything."

So what's the other possibility?

"I hate to say it, but the other possibility is Nestor may be right. There's a good chance Virgil was killed, and whoever did it wanted to get rid of the evidence."

That one gets my vote.

"I'm leaning that way too." James removed the VR hood and thumbed through the pile of folders on his desk. "I haven't found anything that leads me to believe Virgil would take off like that. In fact, all of the interviews I've read tell me he had every reason to stay."

What about his partner, Emery Lewis? He said he was out here on Saturday, but there's no sign of his tracks either.

"That doesn't surprise me. Lewis said Virgil was still here when he left. The scene would have been cleaned up after that."

Maybe Lewis is the one that did it.

"I considered that, but there's no motive. I don't see what Lewis would have gained by Virgil's disappearance. It killed the whole operation and there was no insurance payout. If anything, he *lost* money because of it."

Money isn't always the motivation for murder.

"True, so let's say Emery Lewis killed Virgil for some other reason. Why would he clean up all the evidence that he was ever there, and then tell the police he had been at the scene?"

Maybe he's not that smart.

James shook his head. "We're getting ahead of ourselves. We don't even know if we have a crime yet and we're already starting a suspect list. First we need to prove Virgil's dead."

So, where's the body? And his truck never turned up either.

"That's another thing that doesn't fit." James pulled a map out of one of the folders. "Virgil's camp was a long way out in the middle of nowhere. If someone killed him, they couldn't have walked out there to do it. The killer had to have a vehicle. So, how could one person get both cars back into town? That would have taken some planning, or at the very least, a second person."

The only other vehicle out there was that backhoe, and I doubt they drove it all the way from town. I'll bet it came out on a trailer. Somebody could've used that trailer to haul the truck back into town.

"Maybe, but they'd be taking an awful big chance driving out of there with it. Based on the pictures I saw in the file, Virgil's truck was pretty easy to recognize. It had the bed and one of the front fenders replaced after an accident. They were never repainted to match the rest of the body. In a small town like that, someone could have easily spotted it."

I don't know, then . . . maybe they just shoved it off into a canyon.

"Detective Alexander and his team searched the area. It would have been found." James put the VR display on again and scanned the horizon. "There has to be something else we're missing."

Well, I'm out of ideas. Maybe somebody just fired up the tractor, dug a big-ass hole in the ground, and shoved the entire mess in.

"That's it!" James stood up and ripped off the headgear. "Virgil *and* his truck are probably buried somewhere out there!"

I was kidding, Jimmy. That was sarcasm.

"No, it makes total sense. That would explain everything."

Everything, except who did it.

"But if we can locate where things are buried, we might find the answer to that question as well."

Look around, Jimmy. That's a lot of territory to cover. If Virgil is in a hole somewhere in all that brush, it's going to be impossible to find him . . . especially after this long.

"I agree it's a long shot, but I may have a way to put the odds a little more in our favor."

James pulled his cell phone out and dialed. "I think it's time to call Deputy Yazzi."

Chapter 7

James tried to nap, unsuccessfully, in the passenger seat as Nestor guided his SUV down the twin ruts that made up the road. A small herd of antelope grazed near a cattle pond in the early morning twilight, unfazed by the passing vehicle. Will and Sarah watched the sunrise from the backseat and talked in low tones.

"Did Nestor finally ask for your help, too?"

Will shook his head. "Nah, I think I still annoy him."

Sarah smiled. "Then why did you volunteer to get up early and give up your weekend to come out here? You don't exactly strike me as a morning person."

"Usually I'm not, but the last time Jimmy decided to go off into the hills looking for something, it didn't end well." Will patted the gun tucked into the shoulder holster under his jacket. "I figured he could use the backup."

"And you didn't think Nestor could handle it alone?"

"I'm sure he has things under control, but Mom would kill me if I let anything happen to Jimmy. She still blames me for getting him involved in police business in the first place, and now Yazzi's actually *paying* him for it. Will yawned and stretched his arm across the back of the seat. "I was a little surprised to see you here, too."

"Nice try." Sarah brushed his hand off her shoulder. "Did you learn that move in high school?"

Will pulled his arm back. "Sorry . . ."

"I've been looking into this case off and on for the last couple of years and didn't make any headway at all." Sarah motioned toward the front seat. "Your brother's only had it a little over two weeks and he's already piqued Nestor's interest enough to get him all the way out here. I'm curious about what he came up with."

"Me, too. He didn't talk a whole lot on the way up here. Of course, I didn't give him much of a chance. I slept most of the way." Will raised his voice as he poked James in the back of the neck. "Hey, Jimmy, when are you gonna let us know what you found?"

James roused and swatted at Will's hand. "I'll explain everything when we get there. The place where Virgil was camped is right up the road. I just hope the sun doesn't get too high before we reach the site."

"Don't worry, Stray Dog." Nestor looked to the east as a ray of sunlight spilled over the horizon. "If we don't find what we're looking for this morning, we'll stick around until the afternoon shadows grow long."

"Unbelievable," Will harrumphed. "Yazzi, can't you just tell time with a watch like the rest of us?"

"He's not talking about the time." James pointed at the bushes next to the road. "Shadows are longer in the early morning and late afternoon. It helps create contrast and makes the topography stand out. In the middle of the day, everything will look flat from above."

"From above? Okay, now I'm really confused." Will looked at Sarah and shrugged. "Do you have any idea what he's talking about?"

"I understand the concept, but I don't know how he plans to apply it." Sarah pointed over her shoulder. "I'm guessing it has something to do with those cases in the back."

Will twisted around and eyed the black suitcases. "Yeah, what's in the luggage, Jimmy? You got some kind of jetpack in there?"

"Be patient, Packrat." Nestor made eye contact with Will in the rear view mirror. "Stray Dog has a solid theory, and an interesting way to test it."

Will was undeterred. "Come on, Jimmy, you gotta tell us *something*."

"It'll be easier to show you once we get

there."

"That would be now." Nestor brought the truck to a stop. "We're here, Stray Dog. Where do want to start?"

"Already?" James sat up, lowered his window and surveyed the cold landscape. "This doesn't look anything like the pictures."

"Weather reshapes the land," Nestor replied. "Seasons come and go. Trees grow. The grass dies and is reborn in the spring. Things change in fourteen years."

"Do you remember where the tools and the tractor were?"

"Right up here." Nestor nodded and pulled forward another twenty yards. "I've been out here over a dozen times since he disappeared. I can still recall exactly where everything was located."

"Then I guess we should get started."

James opened the door and stepped out into the frigid morning air. He walked around to the back of the SUV and lifted the hatch. Will and Sarah were right on his heals, but Nestor didn't follow. Instead, he stepped around the front of the truck and faced the sunrise. Closing his eyes, he held out his hands, palms up, and took in a deep breath. James stopped what he was doing and watched as Nestor mumbled something under his breath. He brought his hands back down and exhaled as he bowed his head, and then turned to join the others.

"Are you ready, Stray Dog?"

"As soon as I get my computer booted up." James pulled his laptop out of a backpack, opened it, and hit the power button. "If it's not too personal, can I ask what you were doing over there? It looked like you were praying."

"I was talking to Virgil," Nestor replied. "I wanted him to know we're coming for him. I asked his spirit to help guide us to where his body lays."

"You don't think he's buried in this area, do you?" Will took a few steps off the road. The dry grass crunched under his boots as he scanned the countryside. "If he's out here, I hope his spirit can narrow things down a little. We've got a whole lot of ground to cover."

James unpacked the VR hardware and plugged it into a USB port on the laptop. "I don't know if it was Virgil telling me where to look, but I found something yesterday. I think I know which direction to start."

"You built your time machine!" Sarah eyed the VR display as James brought the image up on the computer screen. "This is brilliant!"

"Time machine?" Will scratched his head. "It looks like some kind of video game to me."

"This is the same kind of hardware they use

for first person shooter games." James clicked a few keys. "The software is where the real innovation comes in."

"You loaded all of the photos they took here and it made one continuous image out of them?" Sarah leaned over and squinted at the laptop's screen. "That's some NASA level technology."

"It wasn't quite that easy, but you have the basic idea. It's similar to how they handled the images from the Mars rovers. The difference is that these pictures weren't taken from a fixed location. They were all over the place, and at different angles and distances. They had to be warped and resized to match things up." James handed her the VR display. "Go ahead and try it, Dr. O'Donnell. I'll calibrate the image so you'll be looking the same direction you're facing in the real world."

James made the adjustments and stepped out of the way. Sarah had an enormous smile on her face as she slipped the display over her head. She slowly rotated in place, her jaw dropping lower and lower until her mouth was completely open. After making a full circle, she stopped. Sarah was facing directly at Will and looking down at his boots.

"I've seen these so many times, but never like this!"

Will snickered. "You know what they say

about the size of a man's foot . . ."

Sarah pulled the hood off and saw where her eyes had settled. "That it's never too big to fit in his mouth? I was talking about the tools."

Will stifled a laugh. "Too easy—I won't go there."

Sarah shot him a look. "Good call." She turned her attention back to James. "So what did you find? Have we been missing something?"

"Look at the display again and I'll show you." James panned the image until the tractor was in the middle of the screen. "Look behind the tractor. There are no tracks."

Sarah held the VR hood over her eyes. "Okay, I can see that. If it hadn't been moved for a while the wind could have wiped them out."

"Look under it." James zoomed in on the ground. "There are several fresh tracks."

"Oh, wow. I never noticed that before." She handed the display to Will. "Take a look at this."

Will pressed his face into hood. "So, the backhoe was moved and then the tracks were wiped out." He handed the hardware back to James. "Somebody wanted it to look like it had been there for a while, but they missed a spot."

"They cleaned up the area everywhere else," James replied. "No tracks of any kind, in or out."

"I think I see where you're going with this." Will dug the toe of his boot into the loose dirt. "You think somebody used that hoe to bury Yazzi's buddy out here, truck and all."

Nestor gave a nod. "It fits, and the equipment to do it was right under our noses the whole time."

Will scanned the mesa again. "Jimmy, you said you had a way to narrow down the search area, right?"

"I do." James moved the image on the laptop again. "If you look at this area over here, the grass is knocked down in several places. I think that's where the tractor left the road. The tracks may have been wiped out, but there was no way to put the grass back up."

"Unbelievable.' Sarah squinted at the screen. "How did I miss that?"

"The spots were in separate photos," James pointed out. "The pattern didn't show up clearly until the images were stitched together in the software."

"I'm surprised Alexander and his team missed it." Will glanced at Nestor. "He wasn't working off old pictures, he was actually out here—and that guy's more anal retentive than Jimmy."

"His job was to document the scene and

collect the evidence," Nestor replied. "Not interpret it."

"Didn't they also do a search of the area?" Will asked. "You'd think somebody might have noticed a fresh patch of disturbed ground, especially one big enough to bury a damn truck."

"They searched between here and the work site down by the river, then into the canyon to the west." Nestor pointed toward the sunrise. "The grass is knocked down to the east."

"Okay, so let's say you're right and we only have to search that direction. That still leaves a lot of territory to cover." Will turned to his brother. "How do you plan on finding a hole in the ground that was filled in a decade and a half ago?"

James smiled and laid his hand on the biggest case. "That's why I brought this."

Chapter 8

James flipped the latches on the large, black case and lifted the top. Will elbowed past Nestor and leaned over his brother's shoulder to get a better look at the contents.

"What the hell?" He eyed the collection of hardware and electronics neatly packed into their contoured holes in the foam filled interior. "I was kidding when I asked if you brought a jetpack, but—"

"It's a video drone." James held up the main body of the craft and rotated it around in the air. "I've wanted one of these since I wrote about the advances in the technology. This was the perfect excuse to buy one."

"I know how that works," Will replied. "Every time Jen asks Donny to fix something around the house, he uses that to justify buying some power tool. Do you know how to fly this thing?"

"I've been practicing, but this one almost flies itself. It's been less than a week, and I already have pretty good control of it—at least good enough to use it out here where there's nothing to run into once I get it airborne."

"What happens if you lose control or it goes out of range?" Will reached for the transmitter, but stopped when he felt a hand grab his sleeve from behind. He turned so see Nestor frowning and shaking his head.

"Don't touch."

"It has GPS and autopilot," James replied, screwing together parts and plugging in wires. "This one has a range of over half a mile, but if it loses signal for any reason it automatically returns to the spot where it took off."

"Incredible." Sarah watched closely as James continued assembling the hardware. "Now I understand what you meant when you talked about seeing the terrain from above, but I'm still not sure how you plan to figure out where the truck might be buried."

"I'm going to use this to look for sinkholes." James attached the gimbaled camera module to the underside of the drone. "If something the size of a pickup was buried out here, the soil has to have settled some over the years."

Will scratched his head. "I think I get the whole shadow thing now. If the ground has settled, the shadow formed by the depression should make it stand out, but why the fancy flying machine? Can't we just search on foot?"

"Stray Dog can cover more ground in less time with this," Nestor replied.

"And it'll be easier to see the shadow

patterns from above," James added.

Will motioned toward the vast mesa. "There could be hundreds of sinkholes around here. How are you gonna know which is the right one?"

"Actually, there shouldn't be too many." Sarah pointed at a shelf of exposed rock across the canyon. "Sinkholes usually occur in limestone or softer soils. There is a limestone layer below us, but the top of this plateau is a volcanic lava flow. It's pretty solid."

"And natural sinkholes are usually round," James pointed out. "A hole dug to bury a truck is more likely to be rectangular and have squared off corners."

"So, how do you see the video?" Will pointed at the VR display they had used earlier. "Do you watch it through the same setup we used for the panorama?"

"No, it has its own dedicated headset." James opened a compartment in the top of the case and pulled out a second VR display. The hardware appeared similar, but less bulky. "It streams the video wirelessly to this one. If you want, I can plug the other headset into the auxiliary port so a second person can watch."

"Two sets of eyes are better than one." Nestor motioned toward Will and Sarah. "The three of us can trade off searching so you can concentrate on flying the drone."

"A bird's eye view without leaving the ground?" Will grinned. "Sign me up. How long can that thing stay airborne?"

"About twenty-five minutes, if it's not fighting too much wind." James pulled out three extra battery packs. "Between these and the one already in it, we'll have almost two hours of flight time."

Nestor noted the position of the sun. "In two hours, the shadows will be getting much shorter. If we don't find anything by then, you can recharge the batteries with the truck and try again this evening."

"That should work out fine," James replied. "It only takes about two hours to get a full charge in each one. The sun should be low enough by the time they're all ready."

"This is gonna be so cool." Will paced back and forth like an expectant father while James finished assembling the drone. "How long until you get that thing off the ground?"

Nestor crossed his arms and shot Will a look. "Stop acting like a child and let your brother work."

Sarah grabbed Will by the shoulders and pointed him toward the other side of the truck.

"Grab those camp chairs out of the back and come with me, Pack-mule."

Will puffed out his chest. "That's Packrat to you, Red Squirrel."

Will retrieved the chairs and fell in behind Sarah as she headed up the road. She stopped when they reached the spot where the grass had been knocked down in the panoramic image.

"This is probably where he'll want to start. Let's set up here."

Will dropped the chairs and started unfolding them. "I don't know about you, but I don't think I'm gonna be able to sit down. This is some pretty exciting stuff."

"You'll want to be seated when he takes off. It might be a little disorienting until you get used to it." Sarah pointed at his head. "The signals between your visual cortex and your inner-ear are going to be confused. Your brain will perceive motion, but won't be getting the matching physical input."

"So, what happens then?"

"Most people lose their balance and fall over." Sarah teetered on one foot and then dropped into a chair.

"Sounds like motion sickness. I'm pretty sure I can handle it." Will sat down next to her. "I went through amphibious training in the army and I've spent a lot of time on my brother's boat—never had a problem yet."

"Believe me, this is different." James walked up and set the drone on the ground a few yards away. "I'm fine on Donny's boat, but the first time I flew this in VR mode I almost threw up. It took some getting used to."

"I'm a little tougher than you, Jimmy."

"We'll see." Nestor handed Will the VR display. "You go first."

Will took it and stood up. "Okay, Jimmy, where do I plug this thing in?"

"Right here." James plugged one end of a cord into the drone's dedicated display and handed the other end to Will. "Plug this in and have a seat."

"That's okay, I'll stand." Will connected the cord and pulled the headset over his eyes.

"Suit yourself." James took a seat before donning his display. "Here we go."

He hit a button on the top of the headset. Both displays lit up with an image from the drone's point of view.

"Hey! I can see myself." Will waved his arms in the air. "When do we take off?"

"Right now."

James flipped a switch and the drone came to life. He gently moved one of the joysticks on the controller forward. The aircraft lifted off the ground and drifted to one side as it ascended. James made a small adjustment to the trim control. The drone stopped drifting and continued straight up until it reached an altitude of fifty feet, then held its position. He adjusted the camera angle downward and spun the drone around 180 degrees.

A heavy THUD cut through the morning quiet. James lifted his VR display just in time to see Nestor and Sarah helping Will up off the ground and into a chair. James grinned and stifled a laugh, then lowered his display and turned his attention back to the machine hovering overhead. Sarah removed the hardware from Will's head, sat down next to him, and placed it on her own.

"I'll take the first shift, tough guy. You sit still until you get your land-legs back."

"I'm fine now." Will rubbed his eyes. "Give me another shot."

"You already had your chance. You're at the back of the line now." Nestor handed him a bottle of water. "Relax and drink this."

"Okay, let's try this again." James increased the altitude to 150 feet and accelerated the drone forward. "You know what you're looking for, right?"

Sarah nodded and gripped the arms of her

chair. "Shadow patterns that indicate sinkholes, especially squared-off ones."

"Exactly. I'm also recording the video. We can review it later to see if we missed anything."

"What do you want me to do if I see one?"

"Call it out," James replied. "I'll hover over it and mark the GPS coordinates so we can locate it when we go out on foot."

For the next twenty-five minutes, James flew a crisscross pattern to the north and east of their position, working farther away with each pass. He paused twice to mark spots where the shadows formed promising patterns. Eventually the drone sensed a low battery and automatically returned, making a perfect landing not two feet from where it took off. Sarah pulled off her headset and handed it to James.

"That was incredible." She put her hand on her stomach. "It was a little like being on a rollercoaster at first, but once I got used to it . . . wow!"

"It is an amazing feeling." James retrieved the drone and sat back down. "Well, *after* you get over the nausea."

Nestor handed James a fresh battery. "How long until you're ready to go back up?"

"It only takes a couple of minutes to change the battery and memory card. I want to get airborne as quickly as I can so we don't lose the shadows."

"I'm ready whenever you are." Will stood up and rubbed his hands together. "Let's get this bird back in the air."

"End of the line, remember?" Nester smiled and switched seats with Sarah. "My turn to soar with the eagles."

Will dropped back into his chair and grumbled as he crossed his arms.

"I hope you puke . . ."

***

A small cloud of dust kicked up and drifted away as James landed the drone.

"I think we're done for the day." He removed his headset. "That was the last good battery. The next one won't be ready for another thirty minutes."

"It's about time anyway." Nestor took off the other VR display and laid it in the empty chair next to him. He rubbed his eyes, picked up his hat, and pulled it down over his salt and pepper hair. "The sun will be setting soon and the shadows are getting harder to see."

Sarah held up a topographical map covered with small circles. "I think we did pretty well today. I count fourteen possible targets. The six in red are the top contenders based on size and shape."

She handed the map to Will. He took it and ran his finger over the surface, tracing from dot to dot.

"They're pretty spread out, so we still have a lot of ground to cover. How do we figure out which hole is the right one?" Will folded the map and grimaced as he looked at Nestor. "Please don't tell me the answer is grab a shovel and start digging."

"We'll work that out on the way home." Nestor stood and stretched. "Let's get packed up and out of here before it gets dark."

James picked up the drone and headed back to the SUV as Will folded the camp chairs and stowed them in their bags. By the time James had the aircraft disassembled and all of the electronics stowed, Nestor and Sarah had finished packing up the ice chest and other items the group had taken out of the truck over the course of the day. Everyone piled in and buckled up as the sun dipped below the western horizon. Nestor turned the truck around and started the long drive back into town.

From the backseat, Will leaned forward and tapped James on the shoulder. "So what's our next move, Jimmy? You got some other gadget that's gonna let us see what's underground in those sinkholes?"

"I'm afraid not." James turned to Nestor. "I don't suppose you have access to ground penetrating radar, do you?"

Nestor shook his head. "Not in the budget, but I do have a metal detector back at the house."

James contemplated the equipment. "What size is the coil?"

"I have a twelve and a sixteen inch. The big one should have enough reach, if what we're looking for isn't too deep."

"We're looking for a whole damn truck." Will laughed. "That little piece of crap Donny uses to find loose change at the beach should pick up something that size!"

"Not necessarily." James made a circle with his hands. "The depth of the signal is determined by the diameter of the coil. The bigger the coil, the deeper it's able to reach. The size of the target has less impact."

"I think the large coil should be enough," Nestor replied. "The top layer of soil will be thinner due to the settling. We'll also bring a long, steel rod and a hammer. If we get a signal, we can drive the rod in the ground and see if we hit anything before we decide to start digging."

"That sounds way better than hitting the shovel handle every time that thing beeps." Will settled back in his seat. "So, I guess the first order of business when we get back to town is dinner and a hotel. Know where we can get a cheap room, Yazzi?"

Nestor gave a single nod. "Already taken care of. The beds are made up in the guestroom and my wife will have dinner waiting when we get there. Mona's expecting you for dinner too, *Dlozilchii´*."

Will cocked his head. "Who?"

"Red Squirrel," Sarah replied. "That's the Navajo word for it that I told you I couldn't pronounce."

"I guess Packrat's not too bad after all," Will sighed. "At least it's in English."

Sarah nodded in agreement before answering Nestor. "Tell Mona thanks for the offer, but I think I'll just let you guys have a boy's night."

Chapter 9

The warm glow of the porch light spilled over the front steps, illuminating the path leading to the Yazzis' front porch. James paused at the gate, eyes wide, and scoured the dark corners of the yard.

"What's the holdup?" Will reached for the gate latch, but James caught his hand.

"He has a dog."

Will shrugged it off. "What's the big deal? A lot of people have dogs."

He extended his hand again, but once more James stopped him.

"It's a *big* dog!"

"Did it bite you the last time you were here?"

"No, but . . ."

"Then it's probably not gonna bite you now." Will flipped the latch, pushed the gate, and stepped through. He held it open, but James didn't budge. Will let out a huff of air. "Get your ass in here before *I* take a chunk out of you!"

James took a few steps forward, clutching his bag in front of him like a shield. Will closed the gate, put a hand in his brother's back, and pushed him toward the porch. As soon as James put a foot on the first step, a string of thunderous barks poured from an open window next to the door.

James froze in place, his eyes locked on the silhouette behind the screened opening.

"You're right." Will grinned as he shouldered his duffle bag and stepped around James. "That *is* a pretty big dog."

A sharp voice cut through the cold night air and the barking stopped. Nestor opened the door and unlatched the screen. Chindi sat just inside, wagging his bushy tail as Nestor motioned for the pair to come in. Will reached out and scratched the panting dog behind the ear as he passed.

"Nice alarm system, Yazzi."

"Yup, and it still works when the power goes out."

Nestor cracked a little smile as James inched past, keeping his bag pressed tight to his chest. The dog remained silent, but Mona Yazzi could be heard barking an order from around the corner in the kitchen.

"Show 'em their room," she commanded. "And all of you wash up before you come into my kitchen!"

Nestor grunted and pointed. "Last door on the right—bathroom is across the hall. Make sure you know what color the soap is. She might ask."

Will raised an eyebrow. "The color of the soap?"

"To make sure you used it."

Will snickered as he followed James down the hall. "And you thought *Mom* was tough."

Nestor followed the brothers, with Chindi hot on his heels. The tiny bedroom was lit by an overhead fixture that looked like it had been there since the house was built in the 1930s. An aging wingback chair sat to one side of the antique cherry wood dresser centered below the window. The chair's bold floral upholstery clashed with the striped wallpaper. Will eyed the bunk beds that stood on the other side of the room, each spread with colorful blankets woven in a geometric, Native American pattern.

"Reminds me of being in the Army."

"Grandkids." Nestor winked. "Stack them up, you can get more in."

Will tossed his bag on the upper bunk. "I'll take the top."

"Um, Will . . ." James kept his eyes on Chindi. The mountain of white fir sniffed at the pillow on the lower bed. "Do you mind if I sleep up there?"

"He's not gonna eat your face in the middle of the night, Jimmy."

"No, but if you leave the door open he might crawl into bed with you. He sleeps with the twins when they visit." Nestor pointed at a silver frame on the dresser that contained a picture of two dark-haired little girls, their braids decorated with colorful beads.

"See, Jimmy? He's just like a big old teddy bear." Will crouched down on one knee and called to the dog. "Come here, boy!"

The beast lunged forward almost knocking Will over, and then started licking his face. Will turned his head in an attempt to dodge the enormous tongue as he loved on the animal.

"His name is Chindi," James said, backing up. "It means devil."

"Devil? Nah, he's no devil. He just wants some attention." Will gave the dog one more good scratch before standing up.

"He gets plenty of that when the girls are here." Nestor pointed across the hall. "Better get cleaned up. If dinner gets cold, I'll hear about it for a week."

Nestor headed back down the hall with Chindi in tow. Will retrieved his duffle bag and put it on the lower bunk.

"If the dog freaks you out that much, you can sleep on top."

"I can't believe you got down there on the floor with him." James shook his head as he opened his bag on the upper bed. "He has to weigh at least 100 pounds!"

"Closer to 120." Will tilted his head toward

the bathroom. "Let's get a move on. I have a feeling the dog isn't the one that bites in this house."

After washing up, James put on a fresh shirt and combed his hair. Will didn't bother to change. They made their way to the kitchen where Nestor was putting the last plate on the table. Mona set a platter of meat down in the center and stopped to look James over.

She pointed to a chair at one end of the table. "You sit there, Stray Dog." Turning to face Will, she put her hands on her hips. "What color is the soap?"

Will snapped to attention. "Pink, ma'am!"

Mona gave him a hard look and pointed to the far side of the table. "Over there."

She turned around and went back to the stove. Nestor took a seat opposite Will as Chindi crouched down and inched under one corner of the table.

"Out of the kitchen!" She commanded without turning around. The dog scrambled backward and disappeared into the living room.

Will whispered under his breath. "I thought she was talking to me."

Mona turned and raised a large wooden spoon in the air. "Keep it up and you're next."

"She's serious." Nestor picked up a bowl, put a scoop of squash on his plate, and passed it to

James. "Let's eat before Packrat gets all of us kicked out without supper."

James hesitated. "Shouldn't we wait for your wife to sit down before we start?"

"I already had my dinner." Mona walked up behind James, put a hand on his shoulder, and smiled for the first time since the men arrived. "You have a good spirit, Stray Dog." She glared at Will. "Yours needs work."

Mona took off her apron, hung it on a hook next to the refrigerator, and went down the hall, leaving the men to their business. As soon as she was out of sight, Chindi sneaked back under the table.

Will exhaled audibly and reached for a dish. "She's tough."

Nestor shook his head. "No, just honest."

"Yeah, well there's honest," Will took a scoop of fried potatoes and passed the bowl around, "and then there's *brutally* honest."

"You never have to wonder where you stand."

"She doesn't like Detective Alexander," James interjected. "I heard her say he has a dark spirit."

"She doesn't seem to have a very high opinion of me either," Will replied.

"She just said you need work." Nestor

78

speared a piece of meat from the platter with his fork and dropped it on his plate. "If she thought you had a dark spirit, she never would have let you in the house."

Will grinned with his mouth full. "So there's still some hope for me?"

"Even the darkest night has a little bit of light coming from somewhere." Nestor passed a basket of fry-bread around the table. "You need to look past the darkness, Packrat, instead of hiding in it."

"Hiding?" Will put his fork down, swallowed, and stared at Nestor. "I don't hide from anybody!"

"Only yourself." Nestor took a bite without looking up. "You like being undercover, right?"

Will puffed up. "Yeah, and I'm damn good at it."

"Yes, you are, but when you're undercover, you're someone else."

"Yeah . . . so?"

Nestor finally raised his head and made eye contact with Will. "So the man you become—Willy-D—doesn't carry the burden of protecting his family, or the pain of losing his father to violence."

Will bit his lip and remained silent but didn't look away. The two men sat motionless, like each was waiting for the other to blink. James squirmed in his chair. After almost a minute had passed, he couldn't take the tension any longer and broke the silence.

"I . . . I've never had a steak like this. It's very lean. What is it?"

"Elk." Nestor took a small piece off his plate and slipped it under the table. The dog wolfed it down in one motion.

"I've never tried wild meat before." James shifted his attention to Will. "Have you?"

"Nice try, Jimmy, but it's not gonna work." Will picked up his fork and pushed his potatoes around the plate. "I've had to deal with a lot of shit in my life, Yazzi, but I've never hid from anything, including my past."

"You have feelings for Dr. O'Donnell, yet you hide your true self whenever she's around."

"That's different," Will protested. "I want her to like me."

Nestor shrugged. "She already likes you."

"Yeah?" Will finally started eating again. "What makes you say that?"

"The way she looks at you. She smiles when you let your guard down. But it fades when you puff up and strut like a peacock."

James nodded. "It's true, Will. I've seen it too."

"What do you know," Will snorted. "You've had one girlfriend in your whole life, and now you're some kind of expert on women?"

"All I know is what I've observed. When you fell down today, you were completely vulnerable." James smiled. "She may have laughed, but there was definitely affection in the way she looked at you."

Will sighed and slumped in his chair. "She looked at me like I was an idiot."

"True," Nestor replied with a crooked smile. "But it's obvious she likes the idiot more than the peacock."

Chapter 10

Will stuck his head out the back window of Nestor's SUV and rubbed his eyes as the cold morning air bit at his skin. He stretched, yawned and rolled the window back up as he settled into his seat.

"I can't believe I'm up this early two days in a row. It's a good thing your wife makes strong coffee." Will held up his insulated travel mug. "You almost have to chew this stuff."

"That's cowboy coffee," Nestor replied. "When you make it, you throw a horseshoe in. If it sinks, it's not strong enough."

James sniffed at his cup. "It is a little thick."

"Yeah, a knife and fork would help to get it down." Will sat up straight and looked back over his shoulder as Nestor turned the truck north onto the highway leading out of town. "Hey, aren't you going to pick up Sarah?"

"Not today," Nestor replied. "Dr. O'Donnell takes her father to church on Sunday mornings."

"She still lives with her parents?" Will asked.

"Just her father." Nestor lowered his head slightly. "Her parents were in an auto accident about four years ago. Her father was paralyzed below the waist—her mother didn't make it. She moved up here from Tucson so she could take care of him."

Will slumped a little in his seat. "She never told me about that. I guess she doesn't trust me yet."

"She's just getting to know you." Nestor looked at Will in the rearview mirror. "Give it time."

James stared out the window and thought about Rose, his birth-mother. "Caring for a parent isn't easy, especially if you're doing it alone."

Will reached up and patted James' shoulder. "I guess you'd be the expert on that."

"She does it as much for herself as she does for him," Nestor said. "In truth, he could probably take care of himself now."

"So why has she stayed?" James asked.

"Makes her feel needed." Nestor swept his hand through the air, motioning toward the surrounding hills. "And this is a nice place to live. She has friends, family, and a good job. I guess her life is here now."

"I don't know." Will watched as the as the houses thinned out and landscape opened up. "I don't think I could handle living in a small town. I'm pretty sure I'd get bored."

Nestor smiled. "I've never been bored here.

It's a big county — plenty to do if you're a cop."

"Yeah, you've got a lot of territory to cover in this county." Will pointed over his shoulder with his thumb. "Back home most of our shit's in the same bucket."

"Speaking of territory . . ." James unfolded the map they had marked up the previous day. "We have a lot of it to cover today."

Will leaned forward and peered between the seats. "Looks like most of the targets are in a pretty tight area."

James studied the map. "You're right. They're kind of in a cluster. That makes me think they're more likely to be natural. An underground aquifer dissolving the underlying limestone would explain the grouping."

"So, maybe we start with the outliers marked in red first?" Will suggested.

"Sounds logical," Nestor agreed. "Good call, Packrat."

"I make one every once in a while." Will settled back in his seat and closed his eyes. "Wake me up when we get there."

***

"Will." James opened the door, reached into the backseat, and shook his brother. "Will! Wake up. We're here."

"Already?" Will twisted, yawned and

stretched his legs. "That was fast."

"You've been asleep for almost an hour." James joined Nestor as he opened the back of the SUV. "I don't know how you do it, but you can sleep anywhere. With Mrs. Yazzi's coffee and bouncing around on the road out here, I couldn't even close my eyes."

"Practice, Jimmy. Between mortar fire in Afghanistan and all night stakeouts with Carl, I've had a lot of practice." He stood up, took a sip from his mug and winced before putting it back in the truck. "Damn! I swear that stuff will make you grow hair on you toenails."

Nestor handed the metal detector to James before turning to Will. "Grab that steel rod and the sledge hammer. Better take a shovel, too."

"One question." Will held up the length of steel rebar. "I know we're driving this thing into the ground to check for the truck, but if we *don't* hit anything, how do we get it back out so we can move on to the next hole?"

"That's what this is for." Nestor held up long pry-bar and piece of chain. "Ever pull a metal fencepost out of the ground?"

Will smirked. "Do I look like a farmer?"

"You make a loop out of the chain and twist it around the rod, then slip the bar through the loop." He demonstrated the move with the rod in

Will's hands. "Then you brace one end of the bar against the ground and lift up on the other end."

James held up his hand. "I get it. The chain grips the rod and the bar gives you the leverage you need pull it out of the ground."

Nestor nodded. "You got it, Stray Dog."

"Great. If you ever need help moving a fence, Jimmy's your guy." Will unwrapped the chain and handed it back to Nestor. "Where's the first target?"

"To the east and a little south." James pulled a handheld GPS out of the pocket of his jacket and checked the screen. "About a hundred yards."

Will smiled at the sight of the gadget. "Finally, a piece of tech I've used before."

"I put all of the sinkholes in as waypoints." James started walking in the direction indicated by the GPS. "I thought it might be easier than using the map."

"You know I like easy." Will fell in behind his brother. Nestor followed close behind.

After a short walk, the three men found themselves standing at the edge of a depression in the earth. Will stepped down in the hole. He placed the point of the rod in the center and held up the hammer.

"Look like a good place to start?"

Nestor dipped his chin. "Good as any. Give

it a few whacks."

Will hit the end of the rod a couple of times, sinking it over a foot into the ground. Another two strong hits produced no further movement.

"Feels like I hit a rock."

"Are you sure it's a rock?" James asked. "Couldn't it be the truck?"

"Feels more solid than that." Will wiggled the bar from side to side to loosen it, then pulled it out of the ground. "The truck body would have some give to it, especially after rusting for fourteen years."

Nester pointed to another spot a few feet away. "Try another one to be sure."

Will moved over about eight feet and repeated the process with the same result.

"Solid again—same depth. I think this hole is a bust."

"Um . . ." James held up the metal detector. "We forgot a step. We should have started with this."

"Little late now." Will extracted the rod using the bar and chain this time. "Might as well move on to the next one."

"It can't hurt to give it try anyway." James turned the machine on, donned the earphones, and did a quick sweep of the area. "Nothing, but this gives us a baseline on the rocks and soil."

James stepped out of the sinkhole and led the party north to their next target. As soon as he placed the disk of the metal detector on the ground, the needle came alive. He moved the coil from side to side. A high pitched sound warbled in his ears like an angry bird.

"I think we found something!"

Will placed the rod and hit it hard. It sank easily this time. He hit it again, forcing it deeper into the earth.

"That was way too easy. Feels like I hit a hollow spot." Will motioned to Nestor. "Hand me the shovel."

Will put a foot on the heel of the tool, sank the blade into the ground next to the rod, and turned the earth. The rusted shell of a tin can poked out of the dirt. "Not a truck, but it's a start." He took a few more scoops and tossed them to the side, exposing more cans, bits of plastic and a few green, wide-mouth beer bottles. Will leaned on the shovel handle and sighed. "Looks like we found their garbage dump."

"Are you sure there's nothing else under the trash?" James grabbed the shovel from Will. "Maybe the truck is deeper."

James plunged the shovel in the ground, but Nestor stopped him. "This isn't Virgil's trash — wrong beer. He didn't drink Mickey's, only Bud.

Let's move on."

Disappointed, James surrendered the shovel to his brother, picked up the metal detector, and silently led the way to the next sinkhole. The detector yielded nothing in the new location—for the next two holes, the result was the same. With each miss, James' head hung lower.

"I really thought I was onto something."

"Don't give up yet. We've still got a lot of holes to cover." Will put his arm around his brother's shoulder. "Let's hit one more before lunch."

Nestor reached over and pulled the GPS out of James' coat pocket and held it up. "Got one over the next rise."

Will pointed off to the east. "There's a closer one over here."

"No." Nestor shook is head. "This one first."

Will shrugged. "Why? Something special about it?"

Nestor handed the GPS back to James. "Just a feeling."

"Lead on." Will stepped out of the way and waved Nestor forward. "I've been a cop long enough to know sometimes you've gotta trust your gut."

Nestor picked a trail around the point of the

hill and down the backside to a large, rectangular depression in the soil. James slipped the headphones over his ears and turned the metal detector on again. He swept the coil around one edge of the hole and then headed for the center. This time, the needle pegged as an electronic scream pierced his eardrums. He jumped back and ripped the phones off his head.

"There's something really big down there!"

"Son of a bitch!" Will made his way to the center of the hole, placed the point of the rod in the ground and raised the hammer over his head. "Cross your fingers and get that shovel ready."

Chapter 11

Detective David Alexander stepped out of the CSI van and smoothed his jacket. He pulled his cap on over his short dark hair, taking care to make sure the bill was perfectly straight. The stern expression on his face melted into a frown when he spotted James standing next to a pile of dirt, leaning on a shovel. Alexander made a beeline for the hole.

"What the hell is *he* doing here?"

"Digging," Nestor replied, one corner of his mouth turning up slightly.

Alexander motioned to a uniformed officer. "Get that guy outside of the tape."

Nestor glared at the officer. The man took an at-ease stance and didn't budge.

Alexander's face flushed. "I said get that civilian away from my crime scene . . . NOW!"

"He's not a civilian, he works for me." This time Nestor smiled enough to show some teeth. "He's Special Investigative Consultant James McCarthy, and this is *his* crime scene."

James pulled a laminated name badge out of his pocket and clipped it to his jacket. "I guess I should be wearing this where people can see it."

"What the . . ." Alexander twisted around and stomped off a few steps before turning back, hands clenched in tight fists. "He's a damn writer!

What qualifies him to investigate a crime scene?"

"He's the one who found it. The man saw things we've been missing for fourteen years. In my book, that makes him more qualified than both of us." Nestor turned to James before walking away. "Bring him up to speed, Stray Dog."

James laid the shovel down, stepped closer, and extended his hand to shake the detective's. Alexander recoiled and stuffed his hands in his jacket pockets.

"Um . . . if you'll come this way, I'll show you what we've found so far." James headed back to where he had been digging. Alexander shot a hard look in Nestor's direction and then followed, hands still buried deep in his pockets. "As you can see, we've only uncovered a small portion of the truck."

Detective Alexander bent at the waist and peered into the hole. "How do you know this vehicle belonged to Virgil Deschene?"

"Nestor . . . er . . . Deputy Yazzi identified the truck." James pointed out a foil square inside the upper corner of the shattered windshield. "And that's a parking sticker from the college where he worked part-time in the maintenance department."

"Any sign of human remains?" Alexander spit out in a mechanical tone.

"No." James shook his head. "But as you can see, we haven't got too far yet. Once we reached this point, we decided it would better to wait for a CSI team."

Alexander straightened up and frowned. "You should have called as soon as you found it. You've probably lost evidence in the soil you already excavated."

"I thought about that possibility." James motioned toward several piles of dirt. "Everything we dug out is on tarps, waiting for your people to screen it."

Will walked up behind Alexander and slapped him on the back. "How's it hangin' Dave? Pretty impressive stuff, huh?"

"It's *Detective* Alexander," he snapped.

"Awe, lighten up, Dave. No need to be so formal. We're all friends here." Will grinned and leaned on Alexander's shoulder. "Jimmy tell you how he found this place?"

Alexander brushed Will's hand off. "No, *Mister* McCarthy hasn't told me anything about that yet."

"Hell of a story," Will retorted. "All kinds of cool tech stuff. Can you believe this guy built a damn time machine?"

"A time machine?" Alexander turned his attention back to James. "What is he babbling about?"

"I scanned the crime scene photos and used them to rebuild the original scene. Then I viewed the resulting image with a virtual reality headset."

"Kid's brilliant, right?" Will grinned and curled his hands around his eyes like he was looking through a pair of binoculars. "It felt like we were standing right there the day you guys took the pictures. I can't believe you missed the grass."

"The grass?" The detective finally pulled one hand out of his pocket and rubbed the back of his neck. "Now you've lost me. What about the grass?"

James pointed back over the hill to where Virgil's camp had been. "The grass was knocked down where the tractor left the road. That's what told us which direction to search."

"That backhoe never moved." Alexander crossed his arms. "There were no tracks around it."

"Not around it," Will replied, "but there were fresh ones under it. The scene had been cleaned up." He stuck a finger in Alexander's face. "Somebody was selling a lie, and *you* bought it."

Alexander's ears reddened as he spoke to Will through clenched teeth. "I assume you're writing a full report on the investigation that led to this discovery?"

"Oh, this is out of my jurisdiction. I'm just here as an observer," Will replied, half smiling. "Jimmy's the one working for Yazzi. He's better with the details anyway, but then you already know that."

"Pack up your equipment. My team will take it from here." Alexander spun on his heels and stomped away.

As soon as he was out of earshot, James glared at Will from under a raised eyebrow. "Why did you do that? You know he doesn't like me and prodding him like that didn't help the situation."

"I've hated that smug bastard from day one. He needed to be taken down a couple of notches."

"At my expense?" James picked up his shovel. "Now that his team is the one processing the scene, I have to work with the man."

Will grinned and tapped the tool in his brother's hand. "Just keep this handy. If he gives you too much shit, kneecap him."

"Very funny." James pointed over Will's shoulder. "Word must be getting out. Someone else is here."

A bright orange, vintage Ford Bronco with a white top pulled up and parked behind the other vehicles outside the tape circling the area.

"That's a classic," Will replied. "Nice restoration, too."

When the door opened, Dr. O'Donnell jumped out. Will seemed to grow two inches taller at the sight of her. Sarah ducked under the tape and headed straight for the brothers, her arms spread wide.

"You found it! You found the truck!" Will stepped forward, but the doctor bypassed him. She grabbed James and hugged him instead, giving him a quick peck on the cheek. "Do we have a body?"

"Not yet," James replied, blushing. "But Nestor identified the truck."

"Yeah, Dave and his crew are just getting unpacked." Will pointed at the Bronco. "Nice ride. Yours?"

"My Dad's. I helped him finish it after . . . um—"

"The accident?" Will tucked his hands in his back pockets and lowered his head. "Yazzi told us."

"Oh . . ."

Will shifted his weight from one foot to the other. "Sorry, I shouldn't have said anything."

"No, that's okay. I was just a little surprised you knew. It's not something I like to talk about." Sarah regained her composure. "So, who's Dave?"

"Alexander," Will replied.

"You mean Detective Alexander? He hates

it when people call him Dave."

"Yeah, I was just poking the bear a little with the name."

"Don't poke him too hard," Sarah replied. "I can tell you from experience that if you make him mad, he'll just work slower."

"Slower?" Will squinted. "It took him forever and a day to process the Agua Fria scene."

"And they have a whole truck to excavate this time, so it's going to take even longer." Sarah glanced in Alexander's direction. "He may be a pain in the backside sometimes, but he's very good at what he does."

Will shrugged. "He missed finding this place fourteen years ago."

"Give him a break. He's had a lot of experience since then." She motioned toward Nestor, who was sitting on a camp chair behind his truck. "Let's get out of the way and give Alexander a chance to do his job."

Will and James collected the tools they had been using and the three of them joined Nestor. Sarah and Will took a seat on the open back of the SUV and talked, while James paced back and forth like an expectant father. After nearly two hours, Nestor stood up and grabbed a bottle of water. He stopped James and held out the bottle.

"You need a break. Watching you is making

me tired."

"Sorry." James took the bottle and rolled it around in his hands. "What happens if we don't find a body? I have no idea where to go next."

Nestor stared off into the distance. "We go where anything we find takes us."

"What if we don't find anything useful?"

"You located his truck with evidence no one else found useful, including me." Nestor put a hand on James' shoulder. "I have faith in you, Stray Dog. When the time comes, you'll know what steps to take next."

"Faith," James sighed. "That word seems to come up a lot."

Nestor nodded and smiled. "I see it's time to start delivering on my side of our bargain. Let's get away from here for a little while."

James motioned to Will and tossed the bottle to him before setting off. He and Nestor walked slow and silent until they reached a ledge. Below them, a narrow section of the Verde River snaked its way though the bottom of the canyon. James pulled a smooth, flat pebble out of his pocket and rubbed it between his fingers. The corners of Nestor's mouth turned up slightly as he eyed the stone.

"You kept it."

"It's always with me." James held the

pebble up to the fading evening light. "I remember every word you said when you gave me this. That's why I figured if anyone would be able to help me understand, it would be you."

"I'm honored."

James slipped the pebble back in his pocket. "I don't know what the answer is."

"If you want answers, you need to ask the right questions." Nestor turned his face into the cold breeze and stared into the canyon. "The big questions are the hardest. Start with something simple."

James closed his eyes as the sound of a generator starting cut through the silence. "When we first arrived out here yesterday, you said you asked Virgil to help us find where he was buried."

Nestor nodded. "I remember."

"Do you think that's what led us to this place?" A set of floodlights came on, illuminating the side of James' face. "Will wanted to check out a closer sinkhole first, but you said you had a feeling we should look at this one instead. Did Virgil's spirit talk to you?"

"That's your idea of a simple question?" Nestor patted James on the back. "I think we're in for a long night, Stray Dog."

Chapter 12

Will's voice cut through the sound of the generator and echoed off the walls of the canyon below.

"Yazzi! Jimmy! Get the hell over here!"

James and Nestor headed for the circle of lights where Will, Sarah, Detective Alexander and several CSI team members stood. They ducked under the tape and joined the group peering into the hole. The top half of the truck, now completely exposed, was rusty and contorted. One side of the caved in camper shell covering the bed of the truck had the roof peeled back like a can of sardines.

Nestor lowered his head. "Is he in there?"

"Someone is," Will replied. "The bones are definitely human."

Alexander crouched down and watched as a technician removed the soil from around a skull with a trowel and brush.

"Take your time. We don't want to miss *anything*." He stood and locked eyes with James. "I still don't know how you found this place. Either you're smarter than you look or extremely lucky. I haven't figured out which one it is yet."

"What is your problem, Dave?" Will puffed out his chest and glared at Alexander. "You need to back off and pull that giant stick outta your damn a—"

Nestor held up his hand. "Stand down, Packrat. Your brother can speak for himself."

James' eyes widened as he snapped his head around and looked at Nestor. The deputy crossed his arms and pointed toward Alexander with his lower lip.

"Go ahead, Stray Dog."

"Yeah, go ahead," Alexander parroted.

James swallowed hard and faced the detective.

"I . . . I don't know why you hate me so much. I located this site using solid logic and some new technology you didn't have available fourteen years ago." He straightened his back. "It's not like I'm trying to take anyone's job. I'm only consulting on this one case."

"So, you did what you were paid to do—great." Alexander glanced down at the truck. "If that's Deschene down there, then your job is finished. You can collect your check and get out of here."

Nestor shook his head. "If that's Virgil, then Stray Dog's job has just begun. This case goes from a missing person to a homicide."

"He's not a homicide detective," Alexander fired back.

"Neither are you." Nestor's face was stone-cold. "Your job is to collect and preserve evidence, not determine who looks at it."

Alexander gritted his teeth. "You better hope whoever catches this case doesn't mind having some amateur sticking his nose in where it doesn't belong."

"He's looking forward to it," Nestor replied with a slight grin. "I already talked to Sheriff Boles. He agreed if we find a body, the case is mine."

"Deschene was your friend. That makes it a conflict of interest."

"It makes me more determined to get to the truth."

Alexander pointed at James. "Does the sheriff know you dragged that kid into this investigation?"

"He was impressed with Stray Dog's approach to the evidence — said he liked the idea of having fresh eyes look things over — might even want him to take a look at a couple more cold cases."

"Unbelievable!" Alexander stepped back and threw his hands in the air. "So you can hire some writer with a high school education off the street and just like that he's an investigator? I don't know why I bothered spending five years in college getting my degree."

Will smirked and held up the fingers on one hand. "Because you couldn't do it in four like everybody else?"

Sarah elbowed Will in the ribs. "It's getting late. Don't you need to head back to Phoenix so you can go to work in the morning?"

Will rubbed his side. "Trying to get rid of me?"

"Just moving the gas can away from the fire." She grabbed Will's hand and pulled him away from the hole. "Come on, I'll take you back into town. We'll figure out how to get you home from there."

"Will!" James fished his keys out of his pocket and tossed them to his brother. "Take the car. I'll catch a shuttle or something."

Will caught the keys with his free hand and gave James a thumbs-up. "I'll leave your bag at Yazzi's."

Sarah pulled Will under the yellow tape, pointed him at the passenger side of the Bronco and jumped into the driver's seat. Once the car was in motion, James turned back to face the scowling Detective Alexander.

"Can I say something?"

Nestor nodded. "Please do."

Taking a deep breath, James addressed Alexander directly. "I know I'm not a police detective, and I don't have a degree like you, but that doesn't mean I don't have anything to contribute here."

"There are procedures that have to be followed and I do things by the book." Alexander stuck a finger in James' face. "Unlike investigators who have been through the training, *you* haven't read that book."

"Have you considered the reason I found this truck might be because I see things differently than trained investigators do?" James stood a little taller and looked Alexander straight in the eyes this time. "And maybe that's because I haven't been taught how I'm *supposed* to look at things."

"That's why I hired him, and I stand by that decision." Nestor stepped up beside James and crossed his arms. "At least a dozen experienced detectives, including me, have worked this case over the years. Stray Dog's only had it a few weeks and look at where we are now."

Alexander backed off a little. "But he doesn't know how to properly collect and handle evidence."

"That's *your* job," Nestor replied. "Our job is to decide where that evidence leads."

"Deputy Yazzi," one of the technicians called from the bottom of the hole. "We found something."

Nestor crouched down. "What is it?"

"Dog tags, Sir. They're on a chain around

the victim's neck."

"What's the name on them?"

"I can't read it yet sir, but I can see USMC on one of them." A bright flash filled the hole as the tech snapped a picture. "I'll have it out in a minute."

James dropped to his knees as Alexander squatted next to him. The three watched as the tech carefully removed the chain and brushed the remaining soil from the tags. He slipped the lot into a clear bag, then sealed and marked it before handing it over. Nestor took the bag and held it up in the floodlight's beam. He closed his eyes and paused for a few seconds, and then passed it to James before standing and walking away in silence.

James stood up and read the name out loud. "Deschene." He handed the bag to Alexander.

"Well congratulations, Mr. McCarthy." The detective's words were soaked in sarcasm. "The medical examiner still has to make a positive ID, but it looks like you were right about Yazzi's friend. Happy now?"

"No, I wish I was wrong." James could see Nestor standing at the edge of the light's reach, staring into the darkness. "I wanted to help him find his friend, but alive. Not like this."

The sour expression on Alexander's face

melted into sadness. "Don't worry about Yazzi, he's tough. He knew this day was coming—he's known for fourteen years."

"But that was just a feeling." James pointed at the bag in Alexander's hand. "This makes it real."

"Do you still want to help him?"

James nodded. "With all of my heart."

"Then put that brain of yours back in gear and figure out who's responsible for this."

James turned slowly toward Alexander. "I thought you didn't want me involved."

"I don't." Alexander cast his gaze in Nestor's direction. "But he does. For some reason Yazzi trusts you and that makes you a member of a *very* small club. If you care about him, the best thing you can do is find Deschene's killer and give Yazzi some closure."

James nodded, put his hands in his pockets, and joined Nestor. He stood next to him, their backs against the light, but remained silent as the cold night air bit at his cheeks. Nestor raised his head and stared at the endless field of stars filling the sky over their heads.

"I never answered your question," he said in almost a whisper.

James lifted his gaze as well. "What question is that?"

"About Virgil's spirit . . . if I believe he led us here."

"It's okay if you don't want to talk about it."

"You deserve an answer." Nestor put a hand on James' shoulder. "I feel him in this place. I have every time I've come out here. Virgil's been speaking to me for years, but make no mistake, you're the reason we found him."

"There's still a chance it's not Virgil." James glanced back over his shoulder at the scene where the CSI team was still working. "Maybe the dog tags were planted, so if the body was ever found people would think it was him."

A single tear formed in the corner of Nestor's eye and wound its way down his cheek. "No, it's him."

James hung his head. "I'm sorry we didn't find him somewhere alive and well."

"You have nothing to apologize for, Stray Dog. I knew he was gone, or his spirit never could have come to me."

"So where do we go from here?"

Nestor shrugged. "I guess we go home and get some sleep."

Chapter 13

James entered Dugan's and made his way to the bar. He dropped his bag on the floor and took a seat next to Will. Carl Stiverson, Will's partner, occupied the stool on the other side. The fiftyish black gentleman sat half a head taller than Will. His broad shoulders took up more space as well. Carl turned his stool, reached across behind Will, and slapped James on the back.

"Congratulations, McCarthy. That was some top notch work you did finding that truck out in the middle of nowhere."

"Thanks, but Detective Alexander may be right. I probably just got lucky."

"Lucky?" Carl harrumphed. "Doogie told me how you did it. Virtual reality and a damn drone? I call that making your own luck."

"But he did have a point." James hung his head. "I'm not a trained investigator, just a writer with a high school diploma."

"Is that what he said? Sounds like a judgmental son-of-a-bitch to me." Carl took a sip of his beer and grabbed a handful of mixed nuts out of a bowl on the bar. "If there's one thing I've learned in thirty years of being a cop, it's don't underestimate *anybody*. Some the smartest people I've met educated themselves. You're right at the top of that list."

"Oh, he's a damn genius." Will grinned and punched James in the arm. "You should have seen the way Jimmy put that uptight jackass in his place. It was a thing of beauty."

"You stood up to him?" Carl reached around and slapped him on the back again.

"Nestor kind of pushed me into it," James replied. "He called Will off when he tried to defend me."

"Yeah, Yazzi's good at that kind of stuff—probably trying to teach you to fight your own battles. Sounds like you did him proud." Carl held up his hand. "Hey Donny! Get this kid a shot and a beer, and put it on my tab."

Donny slid a pint glass under the tap. "Ya both drink for free, Carl."

"Great!" Carl tossed a couple of nuts in his mouth. "Then set all three of us up."

Donny half grinned and grabbed two more glasses.

Will balled up a napkin and bounced it of the side of James' head. "So, you gonna stick with the case or let Dave scare you off?"

James picked the napkin ball up off the bar and stared at it as he rolled it between his fingers. "I think we came to an understanding after you left. He actually encouraged me to help Nestor find Virgil's killer."

"Hold on there!" Will's head snapped around toward his brother. "Alexander agreed to work with a civilian?"

"Technically, I'm not a civilian since Nestor hired me as a consultant—but yeah, he agreed after we found evidence that confirmed the body was Virgil's."

Will nodded. "Sarah told me about the dog tags this afternoon. She's still waiting on dental records to make a positive ID. How did Yazzi take it?"

"He didn't say much, but I think it hit him pretty hard. He barely talked on the way back to the house."

"Did you stay at his place again last night?"

"Yes." James tossed the paper ball at a pitcher on the back bar-shelf and came up a foot short. "And I forgot to make sure the bedroom door was closed all the way."

Will grinned. "You didn't sleep on the bottom bunk, did you?"

"I didn't have a choice. Mrs. Yazzi already had the bedding stripped and washed. She hadn't remade the top bed yet."

"Let me guess," Will replied with a chuckle. "You had company?"

James picked up his glass and took a drink.

"When I woke up this morning, Chindi was taking up the whole bed. I was pinned up against the wall."

"Who the hell is Cindy? She crawled into bed with you last night?" Carl shook his head. "I sure hope your girlfriend doesn't catch wind of that. She'll kick that woman's ass."

"Chindi, not Cindy," James corrected. "Nestor's dog. He's a 110 pound Samoyed mix."

Carl's jaw dropped. "Mixed with what— horse? That's not a dog, that qualifies as livestock!"

Will smirked. "If sleeping with that monster didn't get you over your fear of dogs, nothing will."

"I think we're friends now," James replied. "I also slipped him some bacon at breakfast just to be sure."

"Nice move." Will pulled James' keys out and laid them on the bar in front of him. "I dropped your car off at the house. I was afraid all that fancy tech you brought might get stolen out of the trunk, so I took it inside. How'd you get home?"

"There's a shuttle that runs from Prescott to Sky Harbor. I took that and caught the light-rail up Central, then walked the rest of the way. Missy's picking me up after she gets off work."

Donny put three shot glasses on the bar,

grabbed a bottle of Jameson's off the shelf, and held it up. "I'm guessin' you boys want the good stuff, not that kerosene Mum drinks."

All three nodded in perfect unison.

"Good choice." Donny poured the shots and passed them out.

Will raised his glass in a salute. "To Jimmy! Good luck working with Alexander. You're gonna need it." He downed the liquid in one gulp — James and Carl sipped theirs.

"So, what's your next move?" Carl asked. "You got any suspects?"

James took another sip from his beer and shrugged. "I've only got one so far, Virgil's partner, but there's no motive."

"That you know of," Carl said raising his shot and taking another sip.

James sighed. "I've read all of his interviews. I just can't see where he had anything to gain."

Carl leaned forward to look around Will. "You gonna go talk to him again?"

"What good would that do? He was questioned on at least six different occasions and his story never changed."

"He was questioned about a missing person." Carl grabbed another handful of nuts. "Not a homicide. That puts a different color on things."

"Yup, a different situation entirely," Will agreed. "Tell him you found a body. See how he reacts."

"Exactly." Carl downed the rest of his drink and turned toward James. "You get that guy in a room with a camera pointed at him, *then* tell him you found what was left of his buddy."

"But don't give him any details," Will interjected. "Just get him talking and see what he tells *you*."

"Yup." Carl pointed at the TV over the bar. "Then you study that video until you know it by heart. Watch his body language, listen to the tone of his voice, pay attention to his speech patterns — study every little detail. He'll tell you when he's lying."

"But what if he's telling the truth?"

Carl winked. "He'll tell you that too. Just watch his eyes."

James turned to face Will and Carl. "I've never questioned anyone before. How do I start the conversation?"

"That depends," Carl said with a grin. "You want to be good cop, or bad cop?"

"Like on TV?"

Carl nodded. "I'd let Yazzi do the bad cop thing. You're way too nice to pull it off."

"Yeah, completely out of this kid's wheelhouse." Will punched James in the shoulder again and choked back a laugh, recalling how his brother had managed to secretly pull off the bad role in the past, but not as a cop—as a criminal.

While investigating a series of drug related murders, Will recruited James to play the part of a dealer named Jimmy Ray. The role required James to intimidate a low-level enforcer and another dealer into giving up information. He played the part so well the name Jimmy Ray was now feared in the Phoenix underworld. The name also made its way to the top of Carl Stiverson's most wanted list. The detective had no idea that James McCarthy and Jimmy Ray were the same person.

"Put the screws to that guy," Carl instructed. "If he passes the test, then you move out to the next layer. Start with family, friends, employers and coworkers."

"He didn't have much family," James replied. "His wife died, so it was just Virgil and his daughter. She was about to get married, so there was her fiancé as well. But according to Nestor, everyone liked Virgil."

Will signaled Donny for another shot. "There's at least one person out there who didn't."

Chapter 14

James staggered through his front door, melted onto the couch, and leaned his head back. Missy dropped her keys on the table and curled up next to him.

"How much did you have to drink?"

"Three beers and two shots of whiskey." James rolled his head over against hers. "It's Detective Stiverson's fault. He kept putting drinks in front of me and I couldn't refuse. I didn't want to be rude or insult him."

"Don't blame it on Carl." Missy rubbed his forehead. "I've seen you turn down a drink before. What's really bugging you?"

James slid his arm around her shoulders and pulled her in tight. "It's Nestor. You should have seen his face when they found Virgil's dog tags. He tried not to show it, but I could tell it hit him pretty hard."

"I'm sure it did. The dead guy was his best friend, right? That still doesn't explain why *you* got drunk."

James let a little belch escape. "I guess seeing him that way really caught me off guard. Nestor's always strong and in control. I've never seen him show that kind of emotion before."

"I know he's a good guy, and you look up to him, but he's not some kind of superhero. He's human just like the rest of us." Missy kissed him on the cheek and stood up. "Let's get some coffee and ibuprofen in you so you don't end up with a hangover. Have you eaten anything today?"

"Mrs. Yazzi made breakfast. I didn't really feel like eating, but she wouldn't let me leave until I finished it."

"Typical mom," Missy replied. "What about lunch and dinner? Didn't you eat when you got to the pub?"

"No, just drank."

Missy put her hands on her hips and sighed. "We'd better get some food in you right now."

She walked into the kitchen and opened the refrigerator. James pulled himself up and stumbled into the dining room. He dropped into a chair, crossed his arms on the table, and laid his head down.

"What am I going to do? Nestor wants me to keep working on this case, but I don't know how to investigate a murder."

"A few weeks ago you didn't know how to investigate a missing person either." Missy put some cheese and lunchmeat on the cutting board, grabbed a plate out of the cupboard, and reached for a loaf of bread. "You kinda hit that one out of the park. Something tells me you'll figure this out, too."

"All I did was analyze information someone else collected. I'm starting from scratch this time."

"Not entirely." She started the coffee maker, pulled up a seat next to James, and put a sandwich in front of him. "You still have the paperwork and stuff Nestor gave you."

Without looking up, James waved a hand toward the boxes next to his desk. "I've already been through all of that. There's no point in going over it again."

"The first time, you were looking for evidence of what happened to Nestor's friend, not who killed him. Wouldn't that change the kind of details you're interested in?"

James raised his head. "It *would* change the focus."

"And you're gonna have a pile of new stuff to go through now that you found his body and that truck, right?"

"I guess that's true." James took a bite of the sandwich and rolled it around in his mouth.

"Have you figured out how he was killed? That might make a difference, too."

"I haven't heard anything yet but being buried for so long might make it impossible to get an accurate cause of death." James set the sandwich down without taking another bite. "Dr.

O'Donnell is doing the autopsy right now."

"Sarah?" Missy went back in the kitchen and returned with two cups of coffee. "She seems pretty smart—well, other than the fact that she likes your idiot brother. I'll bet she can figure it out."

"Will and Carl suggested I talk to Emery Lewis again, too. He was the last one to see Virgil alive."

"Is that the partner? I'll bet it was him. They probably found gold and he wanted it all for himself. I've seen a bunch of those reality cop shows and they all say to follow the money."

James shook his head. "If Lewis killed him, it wasn't for the money or the mining claim. Virgil was broke and the claim has never been worked since he left . . . um . . . I mean died."

"Guess that blows my theory." Missy leaned over and pushed the plate closer to him. "Keep eating."

James reluctantly took another bite and chewed it slowly as Missy continued.

"Maybe he pissed off another miner. You know, like jumped somebody's claim."

"From what I've heard about him, I don't think Virgil would *ever* do something like that." James replied. "But he could have crossed into another claim by accident. I guess I should do

118

some research to see if there were other mining claims nearby, especially any sharing a border with Virgil's."

"You should look into both guy's families, too. Maybe somebody had some kind of life insurance policy nobody knew about."

"Carl also said to look at the family." James took a sip of his coffee to wash down the bite of dry sandwich. "Can you take a policy out on someone without them knowing?"

"I have no idea, but it doesn't matter." Missy scribbled in the air with her finger. "His signature could have been forged. Or someone could have just slipped the paperwork in with some other stuff he was signing."

James raised an eyebrow. "You sound like you're speaking from experience."

"I may or may not have covered up a few absences and bad report cards in my youth." Missy winked and pursed her lips. "All I'm saying is he wouldn't be around to contest the signature when somebody tried to collect."

"You're devious." James grabbed his coffee cup again and took a few more sips. "I need to sober up before you trick me into signing over the house."

A crooked smile came across Missy's face. "How do you know I haven't done it already?"

"Well, you *are* driving my mom's old car." James picked up his sandwich and started eating faster.

She patted him on the arm. "Don't worry. The title is still in your name . . . for now."

After James finished his sandwich and coffee, Missy put the dishes in the sink, then handed him a bottle of water and a couple of pills. James swallowed the pills as they returned to the living room and settled in on the couch again.

"You look like you're starting to sober up. Let's talk about this thing with you and Yazzi."

James set the bottle down on the coffee table. "Are you referring to our deal?"

"No, I totally get that. I'm talking about the way you've latched onto him emotionally."

"What?" James leaned away from her and cocked his head. "I haven't latched onto him. He's a friend and a mentor. I respect his wisdom."

"You've only known the man for a couple of months but seeing him in pain has you so twisted up inside that you got drunk. He's not just a friend. I think you see Nestor as the father you never had."

"My father?"

"That's right, your father."

"I don't see it." James stood up and paced back and forth a few times. "What makes you think I see Nestor that way?"

"Your dad passed when you were too young to remember, and Mr. Dugan had already been killed by the time Margie took you in." Missy got up and took his hands. "I'll bet Nestor is the first strong male influence you've ever had."

James bit his lower lip. "I never thought of it that way."

"That doesn't surprise me. How are you supposed to recognize something you've never experienced before?"

"I had a teacher in high school—the one that got me my first writing job. He's probably the closest I've come to having someone like that in my life."

"Until now," Missy replied. "You could have gone to Carl or Miguel for advice—even Donny. But what did you do? You went all the way up to Prescott just so you could ask Nestor in person. Face it, if you could choose anyone to be your father, it would be Nestor Yazzi."

James sighed. "You really think so?"

"I *know* so." Missy's expression hardened. "My dad was abusive and an alcoholic. If I could choose my own father, I'd pick Nestor, too."

"You're probably right." James hugged his girlfriend and then turned toward the boxes next to his desk. "Guess if I want to help him, I'd better get to it and try to figure out who did this."

"Oh, no you don't." Missy grabbed his shoulders from behind and pointed him down the hall. "You're hitting the shower and going to bed. You can play detective in the morning when your brain clears up."

Chapter 15

James rounded the corner onto the quiet street and pulled his car up in front of Nestor's house. A lump formed in his throat and his stomach churned like an old washing machine as he stared at the front porch. He spent the entire ninety minute drive from his home to Prescott contemplating what he might say to console Nestor, but all of those thoughts now hid in the dark corners of his mind. At that moment, the man who made his living with words could find none.

Summoning his courage, James stepped out of his car and approached the gate. As soon as he lifted the latch, Chindi's now familiar bark announced his arrival. When Mona opened the door, the colossal beast pushed past her and bounded down the steps, tongue out and massive tail in full swing. The dog circled James several times, barking and rubbing against him, nearly knocking him off his feet. He scratched the top of the dog's head and down his back with each pass as they worked their way up the steps.

"Good morning, Mrs. Yazzi." James tried to sound upbeat, but barely got the words out without his voice cracking. "Is your husband home? He wasn't at his office."

"He's here, Stray Dog. Come on in." Mona shoved Chindi back inside. "You have breakfast?"

"Yes, ma'am." James wiped his feet and pulled the door closed behind him. "I ate with my girlfriend before I left town this morning."

"Okay, I'll leave you to it then. The old bear is holed up in his cave." She gave a backhanded wave in the direction of the hallway. "Maybe you can get that stubborn fool to leave the house."

James headed down the hall with Chindi leading the way. He turned the corner into the office and found Nestor hunched over the desk digging through a pile of papers and photos. James pulled a folding chair out of the closet and set it up next to the desk. The dog headed to his bed in the corner as James took his coat off and sat down.

"Is that the coroner's report?"

"Yup," Nestor replied without looking up.

"Was Dr. O'Donnell able to make a positive identification?"

"Yup—dental records."

"I'm sorry." James lowered his head and took a breath. "Did they figure out . . . um . . . how it happened?"

"Blunt force trauma to the back of the head." Nestor slid a picture across the desk. "Something with a hard edge—maybe a shovel or some other digging tool. Crushed the base of his skull and severed his spinal cord. Probably didn't feel anything."

James picked up the photo of the skull and studied it. The bone was stained nearly the same color as the reddish-brown dirt on the mesa where it was recovered. A broken line surrounded by a web of cracks angled across the lower back surface of the skull, matching perfectly with a crack in the first cervical vertebra. The second vertebra was chipped in the same area and completely separated from the first.

"Well, at least it appears he didn't suffer." James set the photo down and put a hand on Nestor's arm. "I know that's not much consolation, but it's something."

"He was hit from behind." Nestor looked up for the first time and made eye contact with James. "The coward waited until Virgil turned his back."

"Do you think that means he knew the person?"

Nestor gave a single nod. "Well enough to take his eyes off him."

"Maybe they snuck up on him."

Nestor shook his head. "I doubt it. Virgil would have been able to hear a vehicle coming a mile away out there."

James paused for a moment before

replying. "They could have parked out of earshot and walked."

"That would indicate premeditation." Nestor swiveled his chair to face James. "This was a snap decision—probably done in anger."

"Really?" James picked up a couple more pictures and looked them over. "What makes you say that?"

"If this was planned, the killer would have brought a weapon. Whoever did this used whatever he could grab—probably one of Virgil's own tools."

"You're right. I should have thought of that." James dropped the photos on the desk, settled back in his chair, and stared at the ceiling. "I don't get why you still need me. You have experience investigating murders. You understand how these people think."

"My experience didn't get me anywhere for fourteen years." Nestor put his hand on the pile of paperwork. "Without your skills, we would have none of this. You, me, Alexander, Dr. O'Donnell— we all bring something different to the table, Stray Dog. You bring a new way of looking at old problems."

"I know you're right. I just wish I could get inside their heads like you do."

Nestor leaned back and crossed his arms.

"Who are you?"

James squinted and wrinkled his brow. "I'm James . . . are you feeling okay?"

"I'm fine." Nestor pointed a finger at him. "When you write your travel stories, who are you?"

"I try to imagine I'm Josh McDaniel."

"No, you become Josh McDaniel," Nestor replied. "I've read your work. You have the ability to see the world through eyes that are not your own. Apply that same skill to this case. Don't just imagine you're the killer, *become* the killer."

James closed his eyes and pictured the scene in his head. He saw the mesa as it appeared in the panorama he had built. Virgil was standing in front of him with a scowl on his face and the pile of tools from the photos at his feet. James tried to imagine them arguing about something. He let his anger build. As Virgil turned to walk away, James saw his own hand reach down and grab the handle of a shovel. He swung it with all his might, striking Virgil in the back of the head with the side of the blade. James' eyes popped open.

"Has Detective Alexander finished processing the scene yet?"

"Should be done by this afternoon, but his report won't be available for a couple of days." Nestor raised his chin. "What are you thinking?"

"I was wondering what else they found in the truck. When I did the VR reconstruction of the original scene, there was a pile of hand tools on the ground."

"Right," Nestor replied, shifting forward in his chair. "And?"

"Well, it's not likely that the killer would have cleaned up the murder weapon and put it back with the other tools, especially when he went through all of the effort to bury the truck." James shrugged and bit his lip. "If it was me, I would have put *all* of the evidence in the hole."

The corners of Nestor's mouth turned up for the first time since James had arrived at the house. "So, if we find a tool in the truck that fits the impression, we have our murder weapon."

James nodded. "There were a lot of tools left at the campsite, so if they only find one in the hole, it has to be the one that was used to kill Virgil. Otherwise, why would you only bury that particular tool?"

"You just took a big step, Stray Dog. You stood in the killer's shoes. Keep thinking like that and we'll find the answers we're looking for." Nestor straightened the pages on the desk and put them back in their folder. "What else have you got?"

"Well, Missy thought maybe he wandered

into someone else's claim and that started a fight, but I didn't find anything close by. The nearest claims were several miles down river." James stopped and scratched his head. "Now that I think about it, that's a little strange."

"What's strange about it?"

"Why aren't there any other claims in the area? Aren't mining claims usually grouped together?"

"I would think so." Nestor turned to his computer and opened a browser window. "Mines should be clustered where the most mineral deposits are. Let's pull up the claim maps."

Nestor navigated through several screens before reaching the site. He selected a map of the area where Virgil and Emery Lewis had been working and zoomed in on the spot.

"See? That's what I'm talking about." James pointed at the screen. "All of the claims are bunched together in different areas, but Virgil's claim was off by itself."

"Maybe they found a new deposit." Nestor studied the map closer. "If they hit something big and someone found out about it that could be our motive."

"But if that was true, Lewis wouldn't have let the claim go, and other claims would have popped up in the area." James pointed at the screen again and shook his head. "This is a current map and there's still nothing out there."

"So, it's not a likely scenario." Nestor slumped a little. "If Virgil did find something out there, no one knew about it, including his partner."

"And no one has run onto it since." James thought for a moment. "Do you know anything about how they ran the operation? Like if they kept any notes or records?"

"I don't know about the mining operation," Nestor replied. "But Virgil started keeping a journal after he got out of the Marines."

Nestor pulled a picture out his desk drawer and handed it to James. The two young men in the image were dressed in desert camouflage, with weapons and full packs. Rugged mountains stood tall behind them.

"He had some issues with PTSD after coming back from our second deployment. A counselor from the VA had him writing things down in a journal."

"If he was still using the journal when he was prospecting, there might be some clues in there." James' excitement suddenly faded. "Unless he had the journal with him. None of his personal items were found at the campsite, so they were probably buried as well. The paper would have rotted away by now."

Nestor picked up his phone. "I think there may be a way to find out."

Chapter 16

Nestor guided his truck up the narrow, rutted driveway to the top of the hill. He snaked the vehicle around rocks and low hanging pine branches until he reached a cabin tucked between the trees at the edge of a clearing. He parked beside a rusted old Chevy pickup sitting on blocks. The truck was missing the bed and a front fender and sported a deep layer of dust and pine needles. Nestor got out and motioned for James to follow. They made their way up the stone path leading to the front door of the rustic structure. The deputy knocked and stepped back. A thin Navajo woman not much older than James opened the door.

"Uncle Nestor!" She rushed into Nestor's arms. "I was so happy when you called this morning."

"How are you holding up, Angie?" He hugged her and kissed her on the cheek. "Kids in school?"

"Yeah, and Steve's at work. Who's your friend?"

Nestor put a hand in James' back and pushed him forward.

"This is James McCarthy—the young man I told you about."

"The one you call Stray Dog?" She wrapped

her arms around James and squeezed him almost as tight as she had Nestor. "Thank you for finding my father. We owe you so much."

"Um . . . you're welcome." James blushed. "I'm glad I could help."

Nestor took Angie's hand and hugged her again. "I know it's not the answer we wanted, but at least we don't have to wonder anymore."

Angie nodded silently and led them into the house. The mid-morning sun filtering through the trees spilled through the windows on either side of the door, giving a soft light to the living room. The white plaster walls stood in stark contrast to the warm wooden floor and rough- hewn beams of the ceiling. Nestor smiled as his eyes settled on the stacked-stone fireplace at one end of the room.

"The place hasn't changed."

"We've kept things pretty much the way they've always been." A tear formed in the corner of Angie's eye as she picked up a few toys off the overstuffed leather couch facing the hearth and tossed them into a basket in the corner. "I hoped Dad would come back someday. I wanted him to know this was still his home."

"I understand." Nestor warmed his hands in front of the fire and then ran his fingers over the carved mantle. "It didn't surprise me when I saw the deed was still in his name."

"Steve and I talked about it a few years ago, but I just couldn't bear to have him declared dead." Angie sat in a recliner and motioned her guests toward the couch. "How did you know about the deed?"

"Part of the job," Nestor replied as he sank into the sofa. "I never suspected either of you, but every possible motive has to be checked out, however unlikely it might be."

"Then you probably know we never tried to collect on his life insurance, either."

"I'm sure it's been hard." Nestor pulled a business card out of his shirt pocket and held it out. "When you're ready, this is my contact at the VA. She'll help you through the process."

"Thank you." Angie took the card and wiped a tear from her cheek with the back of her hand. She turned toward James. "Did Uncle Nestor tell you he helped Dad build this house?"

James shook his head. "No, but it's very beautiful. I can see a lot of work went into it."

"And a lot of love," Angie replied. "Mom wasn't too thrilled with the idea of moving off the reservation, but once she saw what they built here, she never wanted to leave."

"Your father loved this place, too. And building it was good therapy." Nestor grinned as he stared out the window. "When he had a bad day he could hit things that didn't hit back."

Angie smiled and nodded. "So, what's going on? I know you didn't drive all the way up here just to talk about the house."

Nestor pointed at the phone hanging on the kitchen wall. "Have you told anyone else that we found your father?"

"No," Angie replied. "I haven't even called Steve yet."

"Can I ask you not to tell anyone—even your husband?"

Angie wrinkled her brow. "Not even Steve? Why?"

"I want to keep this under wraps for now," Nestor replied. "It's not that I don't trust your husband, but the less people who know, the better. Easier to keep the secret that way"

"Okay." Angie nodded. "If it will help to catch whoever did this. Is there anything else I can do to help?"

"Maybe." Nestor's usual stone face returned. "Your father's counselor at the VA had him keeping a journal as part of his treatment. Do you know if he was still writing it when he disappeared?"

"Yes," Angie replied. "He filled several of them over the years."

"Did he have the latest one with him that

weekend?"

Angie shook her head. "I couldn't say for sure, but it wouldn't surprise me. He usually took it everywhere he went."

"What about the older journals?" Nestor asked. "Do you know where he kept those?"

"They were probably in his den. We packed his things up when we needed the room for the boys." She pointed at a door next to the kitchen. "All of his stuff is stored in the attic. We saved everything . . . you know . . . in case he came back, but I guess it doesn't matter now."

"If we can find his journals, it might give us a direction to go," Nestor replied. "Mind if we have a look?"

"Go ahead." Angie walked over, opened the door and flipped the light switch. "His stuff is in the boxes next to the chimney."

Nestor led the way up the narrow staircase, brushing a few spider webs out of the way with his hat as he went. Each swish of the hat stirred up a small cloud of dust. James covered his mouth and nose with his hand to keep from breathing it in as he followed.

All manner of things crowded the peaked space at the top of the stairs. Suitcases, bags, and boxes filled the area on both sides leaving a narrow path down the middle. At one end of the room, a dozen odd boxes with the word "Dad" scribbled on them sat in stacks on both sides of the stone chimney.

"This might take a while." Nestor took off his coat and hung it on a nail sticking out of a rafter. "Grab a box and let's get to it."

James and Nestor each took a box off the pile and set it on the floor. Nestor pulled out a pocketknife and cut the tape. They took a quick look through several boxes filled with clothes, shoes and knick-knacks, setting them aside and spending more time on the ones that had books and old paperwork. Nestor pulled the top open on the next to the last box.

"Jackpot." He held up a leather-bound book. "This is the first journal he wrote in. I recognize it."

James pulled a flap back and peered in the box. "Are there more?"

"I've got two more." Nestor handed them to him. "Check the dates of the last entries."

James read the last pages in each and held up one of the journals. "This one ends three months before he disappeared."

"Then there has to be at least one more." Nestor ripped the top open on the last box and dug in. "Damn . . . nothing but file folders."

"Maybe we missed something in one of the

other boxes." James rifled through all the boxes again. "Nothing. He must have had the last one with him like we suspected."

"I was afraid of that." Nestor sighed and took a seat on a dusty old stool.

James picked up the last journal and handed it to Nestor. "There might still be something in here that will help."

"True." Nestor opened it and thumbed through the pages. "Whatever came to a head out there might have been brewing for a while."

"There could be some clues in here, too." James pulled the box of files closer. "Maybe we can reconstruct the last few months of his life by following a paper trail."

"Piece his life together like you did the photographs from the original investigation." A smile returned to Nestor's face. "Good, old-fashioned style police work. I like it."

"We have his bank statements and canceled checks." James pulled out a couple of the folders. "There are a lot of other bills, receipts, and notes as well. We can build a timeline and plug all of this into it. It looks like he kept pretty good records."

"Virgil didn't have a lot of money—lived paycheck to paycheck and hustled side jobs—so he tracked every dime."

"That could work to our advantage." James

dragged the other paperwork boxes out of the pile. "If we combine all of this with the entries in the journals, maybe something will stand out."

"Sounds like we have a plan." Nestor hefted one of the boxes onto his shoulder. "Let's load all of this up and get to work."

James put the files back in their box and picked it up. "Are we taking everything back to the house?"

Nestor shook his head. "The sheriff's office — we're going to need a lot more space."

Chapter 17

Stacks of paper arranged in neat piles covered the top of the dark wooden table stretching nearly the full length of the Yavapai County Sheriff's Office conference room. James walked back and forth, sorting the loose pages from a box into the appropriate piles. Nestor stood on the other side of the room reading the pages from one of Virgil's journals. He made notes on a whiteboard that had been divided into a calendar grid. Both of the men worked quietly, unaware of the tall, thin figure wearing a gray western-cut suit watching from the doorway.

"Making any headway?" The man stepped into the room, removed his cowboy hat, and tossed it on a chair. "You must be McCarthy," he said extending his hand. "Martin Boles—you can call me Marty."

"Sheriff Boles?" James shook his hand. "Yes, I'm James McCarthy."

"What do you go by? I hear some people call you Stray Dog." Boles gave Nestor a wink. "Or maybe you prefer Josh McDaniel."

James took a step back, his eyes wide. Boles grinned and let out a laugh.

"Don't worry, son. Your secret's safe with me, but you had to know I'd do a background check before I let Yazzi put you on the payroll, even as a consultant."

"And you came up cleaner than this old wolf," Nestor quipped, reaching across the table to shake the sheriff's hand.

"We've all got skeletons, Yazzi," Boles' eyes narrowed. "Not thinking about running against me next year, are you?"

Nestor shook his head. "I'd never make it in politics. Too honest."

"Good to hear." Boles took a look around the room and let out a long slow whistle. "You boys have done a hell of a job with this case so far. Where do we stand?"

Nestor motioned to James, but remained silent. James straightened his back and cleared his throat.

"Virgil Deschene kept a journal, but the last book is missing. We think it was probably buried with him." James pointed to the stacks of paper. "We recovered all of his old records from his daughter and we're using them to try to reconstruct the last few months of his life. We're hoping to find a motive for his murder."

"And a suspect to go with it," Nestor added.

Boles poked at a few of the pages on the table. "Anything jump out at you?"

"We're just getting into it," James replied. "Once everything is sorted out, we'll build a timeline and combine that with the entries from the older journals."

"Have you questioned the partner again? He looks like a solid suspect to me."

"Not yet," Nestor waved toward the table. "Stray Dog thinks we should finish going through all of this first and I agree. There could be something we can use for leverage in here."

"I can get behind that logic, but we need to nail this guy." Sheriff Boles grunted as he sunk into a chair at the head of the table. "McCarthy, you still got all that high tech gear? I want to call a press conference and show the public how we found the victim and turned an old case around using modern methods."

James opened his mouth to speak, but Nestor held up a hand to stop him.

"No press," Nestor growled. "Only a handful of people know we found Virgil's body, and I want to keep it that way."

Boles leaned back in his chair and propped a booted foot on the table. "Give me one good reason to hold off. This office could use some good press right now."

"You mean *you* could use some good press." Nestor stepped around the table and pushed the sheriff's chair with his foot, sending the chair rolling sideways and the man's boot to the floor. "Whoever killed Virgil still thinks he got away with it. That gives us the upper hand and I don't plan on losing it."

"A press conference could generate some new leads." Boles stood up and straightened his bolo tie. "You know this is my call, right?"

"Yes, it is." Nestor stepped forward and got right up in the sheriff's face. "And letting the press know a killer got away because you jumped the gun is *my* call."

Boles took a step back. "You sure you're not running?"

Nestor crossed his arms and stared, but didn't utter a word. The sheriff retrieved his hat and ambled toward the doorway. When he reached the door, he turned and pointed back at Nestor.

"You win this round, Yazzi. I'll hold off for now, but you and your wonder-boy better come up with something fast."

The sheriff spun around, planted his hat back on his head, and stomped down the hall. Once the sound of his footsteps faded, James breathed a sigh of relief. He turned to see Nestor still standing with his arms crossed and a frown locked on his face.

"Are you okay?" James chewed his lip and waited for an answer.

"I'm fine." Nestor relaxed his stance and picked up the journal he'd been reading before the sheriff appeared. "Just needed to let a little wind out of his sails."

"But he's your boss. Can't he fire you for making threats like that?"

Nestor nodded. "He could, but he won't. Breaking a case like this will help his campaign."

"Does that mean he'll be more involved in the investigation going forward?"

"Boles?" One corner of Nestor's mouth turned up in a crooked smile. "He's more politician than cop—always has been. He's good at letting others do the work while he takes the credit. Boles might strut around here like a banty-rooster, but he won't get in our way."

James scratched his head. "If he doesn't do anything, how did he get to be sheriff?"

"He won the election," Nestor replied. "He shook the right hands and told people what they wanted to hear. It has nothing to do with what kind of a cop he is."

"That doesn't seem right."

"I agree, but there's nothing we can do about it." Nestor nodded toward the table. "How are you making out with all of this?"

James pulled the last file folder out of the box he was working from. "This is it for the paperwork. It looks like a batch of assay reports."

"Virgil made several entries about the samples he took and the results." Nestor held up the journal. "We should try to match the reports up to the dates of his comments."

"I think I'll put the results into a spreadsheet as well. It might make it easier to see trends and patterns." James thumbed through the folder. "Wow, some of these aren't just assay reports, they're full soil analysis results."

"More information is better than less," Nestor commented. "I wonder what Virgil was looking for?"

"Certain rock formations and soil types are more likely to contain native gold," James replied. "Maybe he was just being thorough."

James turned one of the reports over and noticed something handwritten on the back. The groups of numbers and letters appeared random and made no sense to him.

"What do you think this is?" He handed the page to Nestor and pulled out a few more reports. "All of the soil analysis reports have something similar on them. Do you know what it means?"

As Nestor studied the page a thin smile came across his face. "That clever son of a bitch."

His smile grew wider. "This is a code."

"Really?" James examined the writing on one of the reports. "Why would he write in code?"

"Must have been working on something he wanted to keep quiet," Nestor responded, holding the page up to the light.

"Do you know how to read it?"

Nestor Nodded. "I might. It looks similar to the one we used when we were in school."

"You wrote things in code?" James cocked his head and shrugged. "Why?"

"Because we could." Nestor took a seat. "I'm sure you've heard of the Navajo Code Talkers."

James perked up. "You were a Code Talker?"

"Me?" Nestor laughed out loud. "How old do you think I am?"

James flushed with embarrassment. "Sorry, I got excited and didn't do the math."

"My grandfather was a code talker," Nestor replied. "He served in the Pacific during World War II. When they declassified the program in '68, he was finally able to talk about it. Virgil and I would sit around the fire at night and listen to his stories for hours. He's the reason we both joined the Marines."

"That must have been amazing." James

eyed the paper in front of him. "So, is this the Navajo code that was used by the military?"

"No, we made up our own. If Virgil used the same system we created, I should be able to figure this out." Nestor pulled out a pencil and a notebook. "The first thing we need to do is figure out what he used for a key."

"I've never done any cryptography," James replied enthusiastically. "How did your system work?"

"We were pretty young, so it wasn't too complicated." Nestor scratched out a column of words in the notebook. "We started with a phonetic alphabet — a list of English words that represented each letter — then translated the words into Navajo. We used those words to spell out the messages."

"But wouldn't other Navajos be able to figure that out?"

"That's why we added another layer of encryption."

Nestor grabbed a marker, went to a blank white board, and began writing the alphabet across the top. Starting after the letter "F", he inserted numbers between the letters, beginning with zero and ending with nine, then continued to the end of the alphabet. When he was done, he turned back to James.

"Now is when we need the key," he said picking up one of the encrypted pages. "It's a number that tells us how far to offset our alphabet to decode the words."

"You mean like the decoder rings that used to come in cereal boxes?"

"Exactly," Nestor replied.

James scratched his head. "What did you use when you created this code?"

"The day of the month the note was written on. He may have used the report date." Nestor flipped the page over. "There are two dates here. This sample was submitted on the fifth, but the report was run on the eighth."

James made his way around the table and stared at the whiteboard. "Which date do you think is the key?"

"Pick one," Nestor replied with a shrug. "You've got a fifty-fifty shot."

James thought for a moment. "Well, he probably wrote the coded message when he got the report. That would lead me to believe the second date is the more likely choice."

"I like your logic." Nestor counted eight spaces to the right of the "A" and began writing the same sequence of numbers and letters below the first. "Take this note and start applying this key to it," he instructed.

James took the report from Nestor and picked up a blank sheet of paper. Placing them side by side, he began translating each group of letters and numbers one character at a time using the sequence on the board. When he was finished, the message made no more sense to him than before he started.

"I don't think that was the right date." James handed the paper to Nestor. "I still can't make anything out."

Nestor looked at the sheet, smiled and patted James on the back.

"That's because it's in Navajo, Stray Dog."

Chapter 18

James reached across the conference table and placed a sheet of paper on the stack next to Nestor. He straightened the pile of soil reports and slipped them back into their folder.

"That's the last message to have its cipher key applied. How are the translations going?"

"Slow." Nestor leaned back in his chair and stretched. "Virgil used different words than our original code. I think I have most of them figured out now, but some parts still aren't making much sense." Nestor passed one of the translated messages to James. "I think he may have used an additional layer of encryption."

James studied the note. Some of the lines consisted of groups of numbers followed by letters; others were pairs of letters mixed with words.

"You've got some whole words in here, so I don't think he applied another cipher."

Nestor pointed to the numbers. "Then what do these mean? It has to be a code for something else."

"Something about this looks familiar. There's a definite pattern." James studied the groups of numbers closer. "See how every other grouping begins the same?"

"Right." Nestor pulled another translation off the stack and traced one of the lines with his finger. "And all the groups that start with the same number end in the same letter as well."

James' face lit up. "I think I know what these are."

He jumped up and ran to the stack of boxes at one end of the room, flipped the lid off of the top box, and pulled out a folder. He raced back, dumped the contents of the folder on the table, and arranged the sheets next to each other.

"These are the maps we used to mark the locations of the sinkholes."

Nestor nodded. "Yeah, I see that."

"Look at the circles we made."

"Okay, but I still don't follow you."

"The numbers." James hammered the tip of his index finger several times on the note next to one of the circles. "Look at the numbers."

Nestor leaned in closer and inspected the writing. "They follow the same pattern as the ones in Virgil's notes."

"Right." James plopped down in his chair and took a deep breath. "Virgil's numbers are GPS coordinates, and they're in the same general area as the claim."

"It would make sense he'd take samples from the area he was working. The question is why would he encrypt the locations?"

James thought for a moment. "Maybe he was thinking of expanding their claim. He could have been checking out an area close by but outside of their boundaries, and he didn't want someone to know."

Nestor looked up. "Someone like Emery Lewis?"

"That's certainly a possibility, but why do you think he'd keep something like this from his partner?"

"We don't even know what 'this' is yet." Nestor held up the folder of soil reports. "If we figure out what these reports mean, that might tell us why he was hiding the locations."

"We'll need to get the rest of these coordinates translated before we can figure that out." James looked over one of the un-translated notes. "Is there anything I can do to help with this part?"

Nestor grinned. "Learn to read Navajo."

James rolled his eyes. "I know you're kidding, but you made a list of the words he used, right? I can use that to help you translate the Navajo words into English."

"You're welcome to try." Nestor handed James a tablet with two columns of words, one in English and the other in his native language.

"There are still some gaps in the list and it doesn't help that Virgil was a poor speller. I've already found some words he spelled two or three different ways."

James scanned the odd looking combinations of letters and tried — unsuccessfully — to pronounce a couple of the words.

"This is *not* going to be easy," he sighed.

"No, it's not," Nestor replied. "Navajo wasn't even a written language until the mid-nineteenth century, and the spellings of words didn't get standardized until just before the war. Some words still aren't in the dictionary — others don't translate into English at all."

James nodded. "I guess that's what made it the perfect code."

"That, and the fact that tone is just as important as pronunciation when you speak. The wrong tone can change the meaning of a word completely — that's why they used native speakers. They already had the ear for it. There was no need for further encoding, so messages could be sent and received with no delay." Nestor pointed to one of the cipher keys on the whiteboard. "Like I said, since we were around others who read and spoke the language, Virgil and I took that extra step."

"So, you actually created a code that was

more complex than the military's?"

Nestor smiled and shook his head. "I don't know if I'd go that far. There were no native words for most of the military terms, so they had to get creative with the language. Even a native speaker would have thought the radiomen were talking gibberish if they hadn't been trained as Code Talkers."

"I thought they used words to represent letters, like Virgil's code."

"They did, and a whole lot more. They used all kinds of things to represent the ranks, munitions and military terms so they wouldn't have to take the time to spell out the most commonly used words. Aircraft were different species of birds and most of the ships were types of fish. By the end of the war, there were over four-hundred different terms the Talkers had to memorize."

"That's incredible." James looked down at their word list. "Twenty-six letters and ten digits don't look so bad now."

"It wouldn't be if Virgil had consistently used the same word for each character." Nestor gave James half of the remaining pile of notes to be translated. "Just do what you can and I'll fill in the gaps."

The two men spent the next couple of hours

working on the remaining messages. Virgil's spelling errors and inconsistent word choices complicated James' attempts to match up the Navajo terms with their English counterparts. To help with the process, he downloaded an alphabet and pronunciation guide for the language.

Nestor chuckled to himself every time James tried to sound something out, but applauded the young man's efforts. He tried to coach James through some of the more subtle nuances of the language, but the results were mixed. At one point James tried to put a sentence together using some of the words he had learned during the translation process. It quickly became apparent that he missed the mark by a significant margin. Nestor burst out in uncontrollable laughter, taking several minutes to recover his composure enough to speak.

"If you said that in front of my mother, she would take you out back and give you the whipping of your life."

James felt his face flush. "I was trying to thank you for teaching me. What did I actually say?"

"Something I'd rather not repeat." Nestor reached across the table and patted James' hand. "Let's just say we need to work on your delivery a little more before you try speaking to anyone else."

James pushed the last few messages back across the table. "Maybe you'd better finish these. I'll start plotting the coordinates we have translated onto the map."

"Good call . . . and thank you." Nestor's grin faded into a pensive smile. "This is the first time I've laughed since we found Virgil."

"I don't think I've ever told a joke, but apparently I'm pretty good at making people laugh when I'm not trying," James replied. "Missy and Will laugh at me all of the time."

"Oh, you're a real riot."

James and Nestor looked up to see where the comment came from. Detective Alexander stood in the doorway with a neatly bound stack of papers in his hand.

"I heard you were back in the office." Alexander stepped into the room and handed the papers to Nestor. "Crime scene report. I emailed it to you as well."

Nestor took the report and fanned the pages. "Did you also send it to Stray Dog?"

"No," Alexander barked back.

"This is his case too." Nestor handed the report to James. "Include Mr. McCarthy on any future communications that have to do with this case."

"Fine." Detective Alexander glanced

sideways at James, frowned, and stomped out of the room.

"I guess he still doesn't like me."

"He doesn't have to like you, but he still has to work with you and show the proper respect."

"We talked at the scene. I thought we'd worked things out," James said as he began reading the crime scene report. "He even encouraged me to keep helping you."

Nestor leaned back in his chair and crossed his arms. "He's a complicated man. David may look black and white on the outside, but there's a lot of gray inside of him."

"You called him David," James commented. "Why haven't you given him a nickname like you do everyone else?"

Nestor shook his head. "He hasn't earned it yet. I only give names to people I like."

James peered out the door. "So, you don't like him either?"

"Not particularly, but that doesn't mean I don't respect him." Nestor sat back up and eyed the report in James' hands. "Anything interesting?"

"Here's the inventory of what was found in Virgil's truck." James ran his finger down the page and stopped close to the bottom. His eyes widened as he raised his head.

Nestor leaned over the table. "What is it?"

"A shovel blade," James replied. "And it's the only digging tool on the list."

Chapter 19

"Yes, Mr. Walker." James pressed the phone tighter to his ear to block out the music. "You'll have the article by tomorrow afternoon . . . yes, sir . . . thank you, sir."

James ended the call, set his phone on the bar, and finished the last swallow of beer in his glass. Donny drew another pint and put it in front of his little brother.

"You in hot water with Simon?"

"I don't think so." James fidgeted with his glass, centering it perfectly on the cardboard coaster. "Freelance writers tend to live in their own worlds, so he's used to people missing deadlines — I think he almost expects it, so he builds in a little extra time. This is the first time I've missed one in fifteen years, so he was worried something bad might have happened to me."

"Been spending all your time playing cops 'n robbers with that Navajo fella, huh?"

"I have been pretty focused on the case. We've been spending a lot of time going through paperwork and decrypting Virgil's notes. It's become a lot more complicated now that it's a homicide."

"I imagine it would, but it's still not like you to let stuff slip through the cracks."

"Missy's been doing her best to keep me on track." James poked at the screen on his phone and held it up. "She synced up the calendar on my phone with hers so she can help me manage my time a little better."

"Missy?" Donny smirked. "Used to be that girl couldn't keep track of herself. Now she's ridin' herd on you?"

James slipped his phone back in his pocket. "I'll admit it does sound a little ironic, but she's actually pretty good at organizing things when she puts her mind to it."

"I suppose. She's been helping Mum get caught up on the paperwork around here."

"She's also the one that came up with the idea to combine the pictures from the old crime scene into one image," James pointed out. "That's what really got the ball rolling on this whole thing."

"Your buddy gonna hire her too? Something tells me she might have a bit of trouble passing the background check." Donny chuckled. "Maybe you two otta hang out a shingle and start your own detective agency."

James leaned back and held up his hands. "Oh no, I only got involved in this case because Nestor agreed to help me with my problem."

"I almost forgot about your deal." Donny

leaned against the back counter and stroked his beard. "How's that going? He got you believin' in God yet?"

"He's not trying to make me believe in God," James replied. "He's just helping me figure out what I do believe."

"And how's he making out with that?"

"Pretty well, I guess. Most of the time I ask questions and he gives me straight answers, but sometimes it gets a little more complicated."

"Complicated? Like how?"

"Like I know he and his wife go to a Catholic church, but he also talks about beliefs from his own culture. It's like he's blended the two."

Donny shrugged. "That's not so unusual."

"You don't think it's strange that he claims to be Christian, yet he still thinks he can talk to the spirits of his deceased friends and ancestors?"

"Ever been to a Day of the Dead celebration?" Donny pointed to a colorful tequila bottle in the shape of a skull resting on a high shelf. "Mexican Catholics do the same thing, but they still pray to the same God as us Irish Catholics."

"That's different," James protested. "That tradition is about honoring the dead, not talking directly to their ghosts."

"But the tradition's got its roots in an

ancient Aztec festival. They're mixing old beliefs with new ones." Donny shook his head. "It's no different than what your friend is doing."

"That's a good point." James took a sip of his beer. "I think my real mother was raised Methodist, but she still put an awful lot of stock in the idea of karma."

"I've heard you talk about it, too. You said you thought karma kept you safe and dumped you on our doorstep the night you showed up here."

"Did I say that?" James smiled as he thought about the first time he set foot in Dugan's. "Apparently, I do believe in *some* kind of higher power."

"Of course, it coulda been God that brought you here." Donny winked and went back to work filling drink orders.

James smiled and muttered under his breath. "Thanks, that really helps."

He pulled out his phone, opened a browser, and spent the next half hour scrolling through pages of research. James was so focused on the tiny screen that he failed to notice the empty stool next to him was now occupied. He jumped a little when he looked up and saw Will's face only inches from his own.

"Cruising porn sites?" Will laughed and settled onto his stool. "The way you're glued to that thing, it must be some pretty twisted stuff."

"That's disgusting." James frowned and put his phone away. "I was doing research for an article I have to get in by tomorrow."

"Waiting until the last minute to do your homework?" Will slapped James on the back. "I'm starting to rub off on you."

"I already missed the deadline. I was up in Prescott with Nestor and completely forgot about it."

Will nodded. "Been there. Sometimes a case gets a grip on your brain and everything else just goes away. So what's the news from up north?"

"We found coded GPS coordinates on some of Virgil's soil reports." James paused and took a breath. "And they may have found the murder weapon."

"Yeah, the shovel blade." Will mimed to Donny to get him a double-shot. "Sarah told me about it. She's checking it against the remains tomorrow to see if it matches up with the break in the skull."

"You still chasin' that lady doctor?" Donny put a glass in front of Will and poured. "I figured she'd a kicked you to the curb by now."

"You and me both, Brother." Will lifted his glass in a mock toast and took a sip before turning back to James. "So what's the deal with the coded stuff?"

"We're pretty sure the coordinates are where the samples were taken, but we still have to figure out why Virgil hid the locations."

"Maybe that's just how they did things up there," Will suggested. "Could be they were looking at some new ground and didn't want to give anything away. Some of those prospectors can get a little paranoid. "

"I plotted the locations on the map and they were all inside of their existing claim boundaries," James replied. "And there were other reports that weren't encoded. I think Virgil was hiding something from his partner."

"That Lewis guy? I did a little digging on him. He's a real winner." Will took another sip and cleared his throat. "You talk to him yet?"

James shook his head. "Not yet. We found all of Virgil's journals except the last one. We want to get through those before we interview Lewis again . . . that is, if he's still around. I don't know if he lives in the area anymore, but I'm sure Nestor has kept track of him."

"Wilhoit."

James screwed up his face and stared at Will. "Who's Will Hoyt?"

"Lewis has a mobile home south of Prescott in a little town called Wilhoit." Will winked. "Like

I said, I've been doing a little digging."

"What did you find out?"

Will held up his glass. "Well, the guy's got a short fuse when he drinks. He started a few fights and got himself permanently kicked out of the only bar in town."

"That would fit the evidence." James replied. "The way Virgil was killed, we figured it wasn't premeditated. It was probably done in anger."

"Certainly moves him up on the list." Will swirled the gold liquid around in his glass. "That makes my next question, what pissed him off?"

James took a drink and thought for a minute. "Maybe he found out about the coded reports. If he figured out what Virgil was doing, it could have made him mad."

"Then that's the key." Will finished his whiskey and pushed the empty glass away. "You need to figure out what your victim was up to before you pay old Emery a visit."

"That's what we're trying to do," James sighed. "We were going through all of Virgil's paperwork when we found the soil reports."

"You said you plotted the encoded report locations on the map, right?"

"Right—and they were all within their claim boundaries."

Will shrugged. "Did you plot the ones that *weren't* coded?"

Chapter 20

Nestor opened the door to the Yavapai County Sheriff's Office conference room and stopped short. James sat hunched over the far side of the table with a map spread out in front of him and several stacks of papers off to one side.

"Stray Dog?" Nestor's voice peaked a little higher than usual. "What are you doing here? I thought you were staying home to finish some work for your editor today."

"I finished it at two o'clock this morning," James responded without looking up.

Nestor wrinkled his brow. "How long have you been here?"

"I got in about seven." James finally raised his head. "I got something stuck in my head last night and couldn't sleep, so I drove up here to work on the case."

"You're running on no sleep?" Nestor set his insulated mug in front of James. "I think you need this more than I do."

James picked up the cup and sniffed. "Mrs. Yazzi's cowboy coffee?"

"Yup." Nestor grinned. "Make sure you chew before you swallow."

James took a sip and winced. "I still don't know how you drink this every day."

"Practice, son—years and years of practice." Nestor eyed the papers in front of James. "What are you working on?"

"Plotting the reports that didn't have encoded coordinates. Will suggested it."

"Good idea. Is it telling you anything?"

"Check this out." James slid the map across the table. "The red dots are the locations of the coded soil reports. The green dots are the ones that weren't encrypted."

"All of the encoded locations are duplicates of un-encoded ones." Nestor pushed the map back. "Reports cost money, and they didn't have much of it. Virgil wouldn't repeat the tests unless there was a reason."

"I had the same thought." James grabbed a pile of reports and laid them out in pairs. "These are the original reports and the corresponding ones that were repeated. If you look at the results, the majority of them don't match up."

Nestor picked up two of the pages and held them side by side. "Some similarities, but some major differences too. It's like the samples might have been taken in different places."

James nodded. "Right—and look at the top of the report. See who submitted the first sample?"

"Emery Lewis."

"Exactly." James held up another pair of

reports. "Every sample that Virgil repeated was originally done by Lewis."

Nestor dropped the pages on the table and scowled. "He was up to something and Virgil was on to him."

"That's what I thought, too. We need to study the reports a little closer to figure out what was going on," James replied. "But I think we may have found our motive."

"*Our* motive?" Nestor walked around the table and patted James on the back. "You're taking ownership of this case like a real cop now. Good work, Stray Dog. I'm proud of you."

"Thanks." James could feel his face flushing and redirected the conversation. "So, back to the reports. Some of the ones Lewis submitted showed no promise, but others contained varying levels of gold, silver and other minerals. None of Virgil's samples showed anything more than trace amounts."

"You think Lewis was getting his samples from somewhere else?"

"Either that or he salted them," James replied. "You know, added the minerals so the samples would look good, but still match the soil from the area they were supposed to have come from."

Nestor took his hat off and dropped into a

chair. "Okay, we have a pretty good idea what Lewis was doing. Now we need to figure out why he was doing it."

"Right." James straightened up the reports and slipped them into a folder. "If there was no gold out there, why would Emery Lewis want to keep working the area?"

"Good question." Nestor scratched his head and rubbed the back of his neck. "Come to think of it, Lewis didn't spend a whole lot of time out there. Virgil did the lion's share of the digging."

"Virgil was doing most of the work? If they were partners, what was Lewis' contribution?"

"From what I understood, Lewis was the money man," Nestor replied. "He spent most of his time trying to round up investors. The weekend Virgil went missing, Lewis stopped out at the claim on his way to a mining expo in Vegas. He was going up there to drum up more cash."

"Follow the money," James mumbled under his breath.

Nestor turned an ear toward James. "What did you say?"

"Um . . . sorry. It's something Missy mentioned. She told me to follow the money, like they say on TV." James eyed the stack of boxes at the end of the room. "You said Virgil tracked every dime he spent, right? We have all of his personal bills, bank statements, and canceled checks, but I haven't seen anything from the mining business — just the soil reports."

"You think maybe the business records got buried with him, too?"

James shook his head. "I doubt it. According to his journals, they had been prospecting together for almost three years. He wouldn't have carried all of those records with him every time he went out."

Nestor shrugged. "Maybe Lewis kept the records for the business."

"Being the money man, I'm sure he did, but don't you think Virgil would have at least kept track of the money *he* put into the business? There has to be some kind of record somewhere."

"Maybe we missed something at the cabin."

"I don't think so. If he thought Lewis knew he suspected something, he probably would have hidden that evidence. The cabin is the first place someone would go. I think Virgil would have found somewhere else to keep it safe — someplace Lewis would never think to look."

Nestor tapped the file folder on the table. "Then why do we have these coded reports? Wouldn't he have hidden them with the other evidence?"

"Well . . ." James stalled out while he

thought. "He may have had the reports so he could analyze them before he went out that weekend, and then he never made it back to put them away. They would have ended up getting boxed up with everything else from his desk."

"I can buy that." Nestor sighed and shook his head. "This is a big county. There are a million places he could have hid things."

"It would have to be someplace close by so he'd have easy access—probably right here in town. Have you checked the banks to see if he had a box at one of them?"

Nestor nodded. "He didn't have one. Angie and I checked that out about ten years ago when we were looking for some legal papers. He had a strong box at the house, but nothing at any of the banks."

"Maybe he had a storage locker somewhere."

"He could have, but even if we found a record of one, the contents would be long gone by now."

James closed his eyes and thought. After a few seconds, his eyes popped open. Without a word, he dug through a pile of folders and found the crime scene report. Nestor leaned over the table and watched as James shuffled through a stack of photographs.

"You looking for something specific?"

"I remember seeing a key ring on the evidence inventory for the truck." James pulled a picture from the stack and waved it in the air. "Here it is." He laid it on the table where they could both see. "Okay, this key looks like the one for the pickup. Do you have any idea what the rest of these might go to?"

Nestor studied the keys in the picture. Some were tarnished, while others were rusted beyond recognition. He pointed to a key next to one with a Chevy emblem.

"That's his house key. He put it next to the truck key so it would be easy to find in the dark. The small one next to that should be the key to the camper shell."

"Do you know what this one went to?" James pointed out a brass key between two rusted ones. "It looks like another house key."

"He didn't have another place that I knew of." Nestor picked up the photo and took a closer look. "Hold on a minute." He leaned back and fished his own keys out of his pocket. Nestor sorted through his key ring held one of the keys up to the photo. "That's the key to my workshop. He used to stop by and borrow tools, or just hang out when he needed a place to escape the world."

"It's someplace no one would think to look,

but if he hid something there I'm sure you would have found it by now."

Nestor grinned. "Don't bet on it. I haven't cleaned the place out in about twenty years."

Chapter 21

Nestor pulled into his driveway and killed the engine. As soon as he and James stepped out of the truck, Chindi came bounding around the corner of the house. The massive beast barked and howled as he paralleled the men on the opposite side of the fence. When they reached the side gate, Nestor flipped the latch. The dog pushed through, knocked him to one side, and headed straight for James. James reached into his coat pocket and pulled out a baggie. He raised his hand and issued a single, sharp command.

"Sit!"

Chindi slammed on the brakes and planted his butt on the cold, concrete driveway. James opened the bag, produced two strips of bacon and held them out. The dog snatched them and retreated back into the yard with his prize.

"I see you two have hammered out your differences," Nestor said shaking his head.

James sealed the bag and slipped it back in his pocket. "It worked at breakfast the last time I was here, so I figured it was worth a try."

Nestor smiled. "What happens when you run out of bacon?"

"I only have two more pieces, so I guess we'll find out. With any luck, we'll be friends by then."

"I think you're already there. His price is pretty low."

Nestor chuckled and led the way to the side door of the garage. He flipped the keys on his ring around, selected one, and slid it into the lock. When he turned the knob and pushed on the door, it didn't budge.

"Haven't opened this in a while."

Nestor bumped the door with his shoulder and it gave way with a pop. He stepped in and flipped the light switch. The fluorescent fixtures hanging from the ceiling buzzed to life, taking several seconds to warm up and cast their bluish glow on the room. The musty smell of turpentine and sawdust floated in the air. Nestor dropped the keys on the workbench and surveyed the space, letting out a long, slow breath before speaking.

"Virgil and I spent a lot of time together in this shop. We built the cabinets and made most of the trim for the cabin here." He pulled a wood chisel off of a rack on the pegboard above the bench and rolled it between his fingers. "Virgil carved the mantle for the fireplace himself."

James eyed the collection of tools. "It sounds like you built some good memories here as well."

"Spoken like a true writer." Nestor smiled

through misty eyes. "Yes, we built some memories — good and bad."

"My father had a workshop in the garage, but I never got to spend any time out there with him. He died before I turned two." James ran his hand over the dusty bench. "When I was a kid, I used to sit out there and try to picture him working on things. I still go out there sometimes to write. It inspires me."

"I'm sure his spirit was there with you." Nestor put a hand on James' shoulder. "And I know Virgil's was here as well. Maybe that's why I've avoided this place. I could feel him inside these walls and I knew that meant he was really gone."

James swallowed the lump in his throat and spoke softly. "Maybe he's still here and he can help guide us, like he did out on the mesa."

"Let's hope so." Nestor eyed the cabinets lining the wall opposite the work bench. "There are a lot of places to hide something in here . . . if this is even where he stashed the records."

"It's the best chance we've got right now." James looked around the shop and thought about how best to approach the hunt. "The first thing we can do is eliminate anything you've put in here since Virgil went missing. That should narrow the search down a little bit."

Nestor pointed out a shelf unit on the back wall of the garage. "That's only been here for a few years. The boxes next to it are new too." He cracked a smile. "Well, they were new ten years ago."

"What about the cupboards?" James walked over and put a hand on one of the doors. "Have you been into these much?"

"I've moved a few things around over the years," Nestor replied. "But I can't recall everything."

James opened the first door. "Then I think this is where we should start."

"Sounds like a good plan." Nestor went to the other end of the wall and opened the last cabinet. "I'll meet you in the middle."

They went to work pulling out power tools, old paint cans, and a whole host of odd nuts, bolts and screws in jars and coffee cans. Whenever James came to a sealed box, he held it up and questioned Nestor.

"Before Virgil went missing or after?"

If the answer was "before" or "I can't remember," then James opened the box and carefully went through the contents. Most were filled with the usual things you expect to find squirreled away in a place like this: pipe fittings, tangled Christmas lights, camping gear, and the like. As they neared the middle of the wall, James found a stack of old cigar boxes on a bottom shelf. He pulled one out and opened it. The box was filled with military medals and ribbons. He picked up one of the bigger medals and showed it to Nestor.

"Wow. How did you earn all of these?"

"Those are Virgil's." Nestor took the medal and held it up to the light. "He kept them here because he didn't want to see them when his PTSD got bad. They reminded him of things he'd rather forget."

"If they brought back bad memories, why didn't he just get rid of them?"

"Because there were good times, too." Nestor placed the medal back in the box and closed the lid. "He said he'd want them back someday when he felt he was ready."

"I can understand that." James set the box on the floor. "What about the other cigar boxes? Are they his too?"

"Most of them." Nestor crouched down, pulled another box off the shelf and opened it. He smiled softly as he pulled out an envelope. "Letters from his wife. She wrote two or three times a week when we were deployed. When she got sick, she didn't tell him—didn't want him to be distracted and get himself killed."

"Did she die before he made it home?"

"No, but by the time we got back she was pretty weak. Mona helped Angie look after her, but she didn't tell me either. She knew I couldn't keep a secret from Virgil. He was like a brother." Nestor set the box down and settled cross-legged on the floor. "Virgil took a hardship discharge so he could take care of her. I stayed in for another year."

"So, he trusted you to keep all of his painful memories safe until he was ready to face them?" James sat down next to his mentor. "That's quite an honor."

Nestor wiped the corner of his eye. "I guess it is."

"Let's check the other boxes." James began pulling out the colorful wooden boxes and stacking them up. "He might have stashed the records in one of them."

"It would be a perfect place to hide something. I never would have opened these without a good reason." Nestor lifted the lid on another box and thumbed through the envelopes. "Maybe he figured if something happened to him, I'd find the evidence when I cleaned out his things."

James continued unloading the cabinet as Nestor began the task of inspecting each envelope.

When James got to the last box on the shelf, his jacket sleeve caught on a nail and lifted the shelf loose, knocking it sideways. Nestor reached in to straighten it out.

"I'll fix that before we put things back."

"Wait." James grabbed the edge of the shelf and lifted it out. "There's something under here."

"Dead animal?" Nestor joked.

"No, something else." James reached in and pulled out another cigar box. He opened the lid, paused, and then handed the box to Nestor.

"Looks like a ledger," Nestor said as he pulled out a black notebook. "And another journal."

Chapter 22

Chindi let out a low groan and settled onto his pillow in the corner of Nestor's home office. James tossed the dog the last bit of bacon from the bag in his pocket and then took off his jacket. He pulled a chair out of the closet and set it up next to the desk. Nestor wiped the dust off the top of the cigar box with a bandana before opening the lid. He handed the black ledger book to James and set the leather bound journal down on the desk before putting the box off to the side.

"You're the analyst. See what you can make of the numbers," Nestor said as he cracked the cover of Virgil's journal. "I'm curious to see what he had to say in here."

James opened the book, sighed, and rubbed his eyes. "The numbers are going to have to wait until we get back to the office. It looks like it's in the same kind of code as the GPS coordinates on the reports." He set the book on the corner of the desk and craned his neck to get a peek at the journal. "Please tell me that's not encoded as well."

"Nope." Nestor flipped the pages until he found the final entry. "Just like the other journals. All clear text . . . well, as clear as Virgil's handwriting anyway."

"What about the dates?" James squinted

and tried to read the top of the page. "Is this really his last journal?"

Nestor nodded. "The start date fits with the ones we found at the cabin, and the last entry is dated two days before he disappeared."

"I can't believe we found it." James sat back and shook his head. "I was sure it had been buried with him."

"You and me both," Nestor ran a hand down the page. "And it's been right here under my nose for all these years."

"How could you have known to look for it? You didn't even know the journal existed until recently." James scooted his chair closer. "What does the last entry say? Does he talk about the soil reports?"

"It says he was going out to pull two more samples before he gets in anyone's face."

"Who was he going to confront? It's got to be Emery Lewis, right?"

"He doesn't name anyone specific." Nestor turned back a couple of pages. "But, knowing what we do about the soil samples, Lewis would be my first instinct."

"According to the dates on the reports, he started retesting samples about two months earlier." James reached over and poked at the left side of the journal. "We should go back to the entries before the new samples were collected. He might have talked about what prompted him to recheck things."

Nestor turned to the first page. "Let's just start at the beginning. There was about a month between the first entry in this journal and the first batch of new samples. That means whatever raised his suspicions should be near the front of the book."

Nestor skimmed through several pages before stopping. He slid the book closer to James and pointed to an entry.

"Here's his first mention of a problem with the reports." Nestor read the passage out loud. "'Just got the results from sample No.27. Show's more gold and quartz than No.26, but the other stuff doesn't look right. Have to ask Em to verify where he got it.' Looks like he was going to question Lewis."

"Turn the page," James prompted with a wave of his hand. "Did he do it? Did he talk to Lewis?"

"Calm down, I'm getting there." Nestor turned the page and ran his finger down the column of text. "Here we go. Yeah, he asked about the sample. Lewis said there must have been a mix-up at the lab—said he'd re-take it."

"So he blew him off and lied."

"Maybe, but we can't assume anything. It could have been an honest mistake." Nestor turned a few more pages. "Here's another entry. 'Em got another good sample (No.31), but something's not right. I pulled one in the same spot last month and got nothing. This one is loaded. Em said he must have got lucky and hit a pocket between the rocks. I'm not buying his story." Nestor set the book down. "I'm not buying it either."

James settled back in his chair. "So Virgil questioned Lewis at least two times that we know of. That had to make him nervous."

"This is still two and a half months before Virgil disappeared," Nestor replied. "If Emery Lewis is responsible, then he wasn't nervous enough to kill yet."

"This is also before Virgil started retesting. Maybe after he rechecked some of the samples, Lewis figured out he was on to him and panicked."

"We still don't know what Lewis was trying to accomplish by spiking the samples." Nestor picked up the ledger. "Time to follow the money, like your girlfriend said. That means getting this decoded."

"We'll need Virgil's word list." James stood up and put his chair away. "I guess it's back to the sheriff's office."

Nestor packed the books back in the cigar box. As they walked down the hall toward the living room Chindi kept pace with James, nosing at his pocket and drooling. James rubbed the dog behind the ears.

"Sorry, I don't have any more." He held his hand out like a Las Vegas card dealer and showed them to the dog. "See? Nothing."

Chindi licked James' fingers, then made a hard right, and headed for the dining room. James produced a small bottle of hand sanitizer from his pocket and rubbed a generous blob of the gel on his hands as Mona Yazzi's voice pierced the air.

"Out of my kitchen!"

Chindi flew around the corner with Mona close behind, waving a dishtowel in the air. The dog disappeared down the hall, tail still held high.

"Stupid animal thinks he owns the place." She turned her attention to Nestor and James. "Hold up, you two." Mona went back in the kitchen and returned a few seconds later holding a bag. "Lunch. Figured you wouldn't be hanging around for long."

"You figured right. Thanks." Nestor took the bag and kissed his wife on the cheek. "I'll let you know when I'm on the way home tonight."

James and Nestor headed out the door and jumped in the truck. As they backed out of the driveway, James took the ledger out of the box. He studied the pages on the short drive back to the office.

"We know Virgil used the date of each report for its cipher key, but what do you think he used for this?" James eyed the columns of odd letter and number combinations. "Judging by the different inks, he made the entries at different times . . . and I don't see any unencrypted dates."

"I don't think he would have used a different key for each entry," Nestor replied. "Too complicated. He could have picked a random number, or maybe one date, and stuck with it."

"If that's the case, the logical choice would be the day he started the ledger, but I don't see any dates at all. I'm not sure how we're going to figure that out."

Nestor tapped the cigar box on the seat next to him. "He might have left a clue in the journal — maybe made a note the day he started keeping records."

"Or he could have used a date that meant something to him." James closed the book and put it back in the box. "That would be easier to remember."

"I can think of quite a few important dates in his life," Nestor replied. "We'll make a list when we get to the office."

Nestor pulled into the parking lot of the sheriff's office and found an empty space. He and James went in through the side door and made their way to the conference room. They both stopped short when they saw Sheriff Boles seated at the table, shuffling through their papers and files. Nestor inhaled and stiffened his back. It appeared to James that the man grew two inches with one breath.

"Looking for something specific?" Nestor said in a monotone voice.

"Just checking your progress." Boles spun his chair around. "You boys have been busy. Are you working on the warrant for that Lewis character yet?"

Nestor's response was short and not so sweet. "No."

"Why not?" Boles stood up and smoothed his suit.

"No evidence to show he's a killer." Nestor pushed the sheriff's chair in and straightened the papers on the table.

"He put himself at the scene." Boles pointed at one of the photos. "And he knew how to use that tractor."

"You know how to run a backhoe." Nestor's face showed no emotion as he picked up Boles' hat and handed it to him. "Maybe we should add you to the suspect list."

The sheriff took a step back and looked at James. "What about you, Boy Wonder? You got an opinion?"

James held the cigar box behind his back and shifted his gaze to Nestor for some kind of a sign. Nestor's expression didn't change, and James knew what that meant. It was time for him to stand up to Sheriff Boles, as he had with Detective Alexander.

"In my opinion, we don't have enough evidence to say who killed Virgil, but we're following a new lead."

"New lead?" Boles turned to Nestor. "You didn't say anything about a new lead."

Nestor stood tall and crossed his arms.

"You can read about it in my next report."

Chapter 23

James pulled the encoded ledger out of the cigar box and studied it. As he thumbed through the pages, he scribbled notes on a pad of paper.

"Judging by the patterns, I'd say the first column is dates. They all have similar characters that seem to increment as they go down the column."

"That's a good assumption." Nestor looked up from the journal in his hands. "I haven't found anything in here yet that would indicate a key for the cipher."

"I already tried Virgil's birthday," James replied, "but I didn't get anything that looks like a real word—even in Navajo. I'll try his daughter's birthday next."

Nestor grinned. "Worst case, there's only thirty-one days in the longest month. You'll hit the right one eventually."

"I really hope it doesn't come to that." James sighed. "With my luck, the key will be the thirty-first one I try."

"I don't think so. You've got a pretty good track record. Your brother, on the other hand . . ." Nestor grinned. "Well, that's a different story. Can you write some kind of a program to go through the numbers? Maybe something that offsets by one number every time it loops?"

James shook his head. "I'm not really a programmer. I could probably write a macro for a spreadsheet, but I'm afraid that would take me longer to figure out than just running the numbers manually. I only have to try each key on the first couple of entries to see if it's going to work."

"I'm sure it'll turn out to be one of the dates on our list. Go ahead and give Angie's birthday a shot." Nestor turned another page in the journal. "I'll keep looking through this."

James adjusted the key to the date of Angie's birthday and applied it to the first entry. "That one didn't work either. I still have his wife's birthday to try. If that doesn't do it, I'll start at the beginning and run every number."

Nestor paused, then closed the journal and set it on the table. "Try the seventeenth."

"Why the seventeenth?" James checked his list. "I thought you said his wife was born on the twenty-second."

"She was." The corners of Nestor's mouth turned down slightly. "She passed away on June seventeenth. Virgil went back to Tuba City on that day every year so he could be with her family and honor her spirit. When he didn't show up that year, I knew for sure he was dead. He never would have missed that day if he was still walking this earth."

James offset the key by seventeen characters and tried again.

"I think that's it. This word looks familiar." He checked the entry against the Navajo word list on the white board. "It's on the list, and it corresponds to a number."

Nestor looked up at the ceiling and whispered. "Thanks, Virgil."

"Yeah, thanks." James said softly. He smiled at Nestor. "I think I'm starting to believe in spirits, too."

"We've been finding a lot of needles in some pretty big haystacks lately," Nestor replied. "I don't have a better explanation. Do you?"

James shook his head. "I'd love to take the credit, but finding the ledger *and* the journal? Other forces have got to be at work here."

"So, we're making progress on both sides of our deal." Nestor's smile returned. "Now we know you believe in a greater force. The next step is to figure out what that force is."

"It seems like every time I get an answer, it creates another question." James held up the ledger. "I think I'll concentrate on these entries first."

James spent the next hour and a half applying the cipher key to the characters in the ledger. As he completed each page, he handed it off to Nestor to translate the words from Navajo to English. When all of the pages were finished, James entered the decoded information into a spreadsheet on Nestor's laptop. He printed the sheet and analyzed the numbers as they ate the lunch Mrs. Yazzi had packed for them.

"It looks like Virgil was tracking everything, not just the money *he* put in." James ran his finger down a column and stopped at the total. "He was investing a lot more into the venture than he was taking out for expenses."

"What about Lewis?" Nestor asked. "Was he in the red too?"

"It appears the bulk of the money Lewis was depositing came from investors." James continued down the page and onto the next one. "His expenses were pretty high."

"What was he spending the money on?"

"Some of it was for tools and supplies, including that backhoe." James flipped over another page. "Most of his big expenditures were travel related—presumably, he was going different places to meet investors to drum up capital. There were several trips to Las Vegas, like the one he took the weekend Virgil went missing. Do you think Lewis was going up there and gambling?"

"Could be, but there's a lot of money floating around that town," Nestor replied. "Casinos are not the only way to gamble. Some of those people are looking for investments as well. Lewis was supposed to be finding backers so they could scale up the operation."

James scratched his head. "Why would they be scaling up the operation? They hadn't found any significant signs of gold deposits yet."

"Maybe they were doing it based on the salted samples Lewis was providing." Nestor leaned back and laced his fingers behind his head. "He could have been using those reports to bait the investors. What else do you see?"

"Anytime Lewis didn't have a receipt to back something up, Virgil made a notation next to the entry," James replied. "Those entries add up to some pretty big numbers."

"How big?"

"I'm just guessing based on where Lewis said he stayed, but some of these hotel bills have to be at least double what it should have cost." James pointed out a rather large number. "And there are several entries like this that are just marked 'cash draw' with no explanation at all."

Nestor sat back up and looked at the entry. "He could have been siphoning off money. That would have got Virgil plenty stirred up."

"I agree." James shuffled through the pages again. "What I'm wondering is, how did Virgil get this level of information if Lewis was the money man and kept the books?"

"That's a good question." Nestor picked up the coded ledger and flipped through it. "Lewis wouldn't have volunteered this information, even if Virgil asked him for it directly. He probably would have showed him a cooked set of books."

"Virgil must have figured out a way to get access to the original books for the business," James replied. "He probably copied down the entries whenever he had the chance, and then added them to his coded copy."

"And then he stashed it in my garage, along with the journal, before he went out that weekend." Nestor set the ledger down and stared out the window. "Virgil must have sensed that things were about to blow up."

"Why didn't he come to you for help?" James asked. "You were his best friend, and a police officer."

"I would guess the reason was pride." Nestor lowered his eyes as he shifted in his chair. "I told Virgil I didn't trust Emery Lewis the first time he introduced us. I said he shouldn't get tied up with a man like that, but he didn't listen."

"So, you think he was afraid you would say

I told you so?"

"He knew I'd never rub his nose in it, but he would have been embarrassed about the situation. I could see him trying to handle things on his own before calling for backup."

"That's not a good idea," James replied with a sheepish smile. "I learned that lesson the hard way."

"Yes, you did." Nestor smiled and nodded. "Did you get that old Land Rover back on the road yet?"

"Nigel?" James nodded. "Yeah, we fixed him . . . well, Missy did. Did you know she can weld?"

Nestor laughed. "No, but it doesn't surprise me."

James turned his attention back to the case. "So, now we have evidence there was probably some kind of fraud going on and Virgil was figuring it out." He gathered up the spreadsheets into a neat pile and placed the ledger on top. "So, what do we do next?"

"Well, we have a suspect with opportunity and motive." Nestor stood up and reached for his jacket. "I think it's finally time we paid Emery Lewis a visit."

Chapter 24

James stared out the window and chewed his nails as Nestor piloted the truck down the twisting road between Prescott and Wilhoit. Driving the tight, blind corners of the stretch known as White Spar was enough to make most people nervous, but the winding road was not the source of James' angst. He'd driven this route a few times himself and liked the feel of the g-forces pulling at his body as they rounded each bend. His discomfort stemmed from the task waiting at the end of the ride.

"This is the first time I've ever officially been involved in questioning someone. What do we do?"

"We ask questions." Nestor concentrated as he accelerated out of a corner. "Just follow my lead and you'll be fine."

James kept his eyes glued to the winding road. "I think it's better if I just keep quiet."

"Maybe at first." Nestor pumped the brakes and leaned his body into the next corner. "But if you have a question you need answered, speak up."

"When do we tell him about finding Virgil and the truck?" James gripped the door handle through the next turn.

"When the time is right."

"But how will we know it's the right time? I don't want to mess this up."

"Lewis will let us know." Nestor finally looked over at James as the road in front of them straightened out. "Watch his eyes. The signs will be there."

"That's what Detective Stiverson said too."

"Carl's a smart man. You can learn a lot from him."

James smiled. "He said the same thing about you."

"Like I said, he's a smart man." Nestor winked and slowed the truck as they passed a bar on the way into the tiny town.

"Will did a background check on Emery Lewis." James pointed toward the bar. "He said Lewis had been permanently banned from that place."

"He spent a few nights in jail after the last fight he started there." Nestor made a right turn on the first paved side road. "The charges were dropped after he agreed never to come back."

"I figured you would have checked up on him too."

Nestor gave a nod as he turned onto a dirt road. "I've kept tabs on him over the years. He's had a rough time of it since Virgil disappeared— crawled into a bottle and never came out."

"Do you think guilt drove him to drink?"

"Maybe, but living under a cloud of suspicion could also drive an innocent man to it." Nestor pulled to the side of the road and brought the truck to a stop. "This is the place."

James looked at the weathered mobile home set back from the road. The trailer's skirting was bent and twisted in some places, and missing in others. Weeds grew up through the piles of junk and warped, weathered lumber covering the property.

When Nestor got out of the truck and approached the sagging chain link fence, a skinny, tan colored mutt ran out from under the trailer, teeth bared as he barked and howled. James slammed his door and stayed in the truck. Nestor laughed and pointed at James' pocket.

"Got any of that bacon left?"

"No, I gave it all to Chindi."

"Check the glove box. There might be some jerky in there."

James opened the compartment and dug until he found a small bag of beef jerky. He held it out, but Nestor motioned for him to get out the truck and come over to the fence. James hesitated, then relented.

"Give him a piece."

James' eyes bulged. "You want me to do it?"

"You did fine with my dog, and he's four times this guy's size. Just move slow and toss him a chunk."

James stepped forward and pulled a piece of the jerky out of the bag. He tossed it over the fence and stepped back. The dog stopped barking, gave the dried meat a sniff, and then gobbled it down like he hadn't eaten in a week.

"Get a little closer this time," Nestor instructed. "You got his attention — now show him you're the gravy train."

James inched closer to the fence and reached into the bag again. The dog approached in a low crouch, stretching his neck until his nose almost touched the fence. James held the jerky out and poked it through the chain link. The dog took the treat from his fingers and wolfed it down. He repeated the process one more time with a larger piece. This time, the dog grabbed his prize and retreated back under the trailer.

"He won't give us any trouble now." Nestor lifted the latch on the gate and opened it. "Just keep another piece handy, in case he comes back out."

James kept his eyes on the spot where the dog went under the trailer as Nestor made his way up the rickety steps. He knocked on the door, stepped back down to the ground, and waited. The door opened and a thin, gray-haired woman with leather skin and a hard look on her face stepped out onto the landing. The lines on her forehead deepened when she spotted Nestor.

"Deputy Yazzi." She spat out the name like it left a bad taste in her mouth. "What the hell do you want?"

"Nice to see you too, Cora. Is your husband home?"

"Haven't seen him since yesterday — took off for a job and never came back." Cora Lewis crossed her arms and leaned on the doorframe. "Probably got drunk after they paid him, and now he's sleeping it off in his truck. That's how it usually goes."

"You know where the job was?" Nestor asked in a matter-of-fact tone. "I'd like to talk to him."

"Again?" She gritted her teeth. "You've been hounding Emery ever since that damn Indian took off with whatever money they had and left him holding the bag."

Nestor remained calm. "That 'damn Indian' was my best friend. I'm still trying to find out what happened to him."

"And driving my husband to drink in the process!" Cora threw her hands in the air and pointed a gnarled finger at a rusting backhoe parked against the side fence. "Do you know how many jobs I've had to finish because that old man got drunk and never came back? Too damn many!"

James finally spoke up. "Is that the same tractor they had out at the mining claim?"

"Who the hell are you?" Cora looked at James like she hadn't noticed he was there until now. "You the latest sucker this guy's roped into helping him torture Em?"

James opened his mouth to answer, but Nestor beat him to it.

"Mr. McCarthy is an investigator who specializes in cold cases. He's been hired to find Virgil." Nestor stepped to the side. "Are you going to answer his question?"

"Yeah, that's the same one." Cora crossed her arms again and scuffed the doormat with her slipper. "About the only thing left around here that still works."

"Do you mind if I take a look at it?"

She flipped the back of her hand in the general direction of the tractor. "Suit yourself. Nothing to see but a bunch of rust and a puddle of hydraulic oil."

James walked over to the backhoe and circled around it. He wasn't sure what to look for, as he'd never been this close to any piece of heavy equipment before. After making a full pass around the tractor, he climbed up and squeezed into the seat. He pulled his knees up high to position his feet on the pedals, and placed his hands on the control levers. James took a pad out of his pocket and made a few notes, then climbed down and rejoined Nestor.

"How tall is your husband?" James asked.

"Used to be six foot even, but he's lost an inch or two over the years." Cora squinted and scowled. "Why?"

James made another note. "Just curious."

"I'd still like to talk to Emery." Nestor pulled a card out of his breast pocket and held it out. "Tell him to call me when he sobers up."

Cora snatched the card. "You mean *if* he sobers up."

As they turned to walk away, James felt something cold against his hand. He looked down and saw the dog nosing at his fingers. His sad eyes and tucked tail made James' heart drop. He took another piece of jerky out of the bag in his pocket, knelt down, and gave it to the emaciated animal. He furrowed his brow and looked up at Cora.

"You don't take very good care of your dog." James couldn't believe the words came out of his mouth.

"He ain't mine," Cora snapped back.

"Damn stray's been hanging around for a couple of weeks. Every time I try to run him off he goes under the trailer."

James rubbed the dog's head and gave him another piece of jerky. "He's probably just cold. It's warm under there."

"Yeah, well it's warmer at the pound."

James and the pup both looked up at Nestor with the same hangdog expression. Nestor smiled and nodded before turning back toward the trailer.

"We'll get the dog out of your hair. You just make sure Emery calls me when he gets home."

Chapter 25

Missy walked through the front door of James' house and closed it behind her. As she dropped her purse on the couch, something caught her attention. Pointing her nose in the air, she sniffed several times.

"Jimmy?" She sniffed again. "What's that smell?"

Getting no response, Missy headed down the hallway to check the bedrooms and bathroom, but found no sign of her boyfriend. As she came around the corner into the kitchen, she heard a muffled voice coming from the laundry room. She opened the door and froze. James was standing over the big laundry sink speaking in a soft voice as he gently scrubbed a wet, soapy dog.

"What the—" She put her hands on her hips. "Where did *that* come from?"

James looked up and smiled. "Nestor and I rescued him this afternoon. I named him Mac. It's short for McDaniel."

"You named the dog after your imaginary friend? You're weird." Missy walked over and kissed James on the cheek. "You're lucky I like weird. So, what's the story with this guy?"

"He was hiding under the trailer when we

went to question a suspect." James carefully ran warm water over the dog with the spray nozzle, making sure not to get soap in its eyes. "They were going to catch him and take him to the pound. I just couldn't let that happen. I felt sorry for him."

"So, Stray Dog adopted a stray dog?"

"Nestor said he was my spirit animal. I think he was just joking, but with him it's hard to tell sometimes."

"Oh, I think that makes perfect sense." Missy reached out to pet the pup, but he pulled his head away.

"He's still a little scared." James pulled a towel off a hook, draped it over the dog and gently rubbed him down. "I think the only reason he likes me is because I fed him."

Missy shrugged. "It worked on me."

She moved slower this time and held her hand out. Mac hesitated, then stretched his neck and sniffed her fingers. He flicked out his tongue and gave a quick lick before pulling back.

"He'll be okay once he gets used to his new home." James lifted the dog out of the sink and set him on the floor.

As soon as he pulled the towel off, Mac shook his whole body, fluffing out his damp, stringy hair. He circled around James, rubbing against his jeans and wagging his tail for the first time since being rescued. James crouched and rubbed the dog down some more with the towel.

"I think he liked the bath . . . and he smells a lot better too."

"You need to get Will in that sink," Missy joked. "He's been working undercover again. When he stopped by the pub today, your mom made him stand outside the back door so the customers wouldn't think the smell was coming from the kitchen."

James looked up at her and laughed. "Come on, he doesn't let things get as bad as he used to. I think he doesn't want to scare off Dr. O'Donnell."

"I don't think the smell is a problem for her." Missy wrinkled her nose and squinted. "I mean, she works with dead, rotting bodies. If he scares her off, it's going to be with his big mouth."

"She handles that pretty well, too." James picked up a dog collar off the counter and buckled it around Mac's neck.

Missy got down on her knees next to James. "You should take this guy into the vet to get checked out. He looks awful skinny. He might be sick."

"Nestor called the vet where he takes Chindi. We stopped there on our way back into town. The doctor said he was a little malnourished, but otherwise he looked okay. He only weighs thirty pounds. They said he should be about forty to forty-five."

"Do you even know how to take care of a dog? You've never had a pet before."

James opened his mouth to answer, but Missy held up her hand.

"I know, I know. You've already searched the internet and watched some videos, right?"

"No, I haven't . . . yet, but Nestor talked to me about it." James reached up, pulled a bowl of kibble down off the counter and set it in front of the dog. Mac dove in, barely taking time to swallow before wolfing down another mouthful. "He gave me a leash and enough food for a couple of days. Mrs. Yazzi cut down one of Chindi's old collars for him."

"Don't feed him too much all at once. He'll eat until he pukes." Missy stroked Mac's caramel colored fur as he ate. This time he didn't pull away. "Give him smaller amounts several times a day for a while. You don't want him to eat too fast and get sick. Once he figures out getting food isn't a problem anymore, he'll slow down."

James picked up the empty bowl. "I know I need to get him licensed too, but I think I'm going to give him a few days to settle in before taking him in for his shots."

Missy tilted her head down low and looked

under the dog. "You should also see about getting him fixed while you're there."

"Fixed? You mean—" James held out two fingers and mimed a pair of scissors.

"That's exactly what I mean. Trust me, he'll be a whole lot easier to deal with in the long run." Missy giggled. "Come to think of it, maybe you should take Will too."

"Very funny." James attached the leash to Mac's collar and stood up. "I should probably walk him right after he eats so he can . . . you know . . . do his business."

"You mean take a dump?" Missy grinned. "It's okay, you can say it, Jimmy. I've heard a whole lot worse. I hope he's housebroken."

"We haven't been home long enough to find out."

"You might want to study up on that first," Missy said with a smirk.

James opened the back door and walked down the steps. Mac hesitated at first, but jumped down as soon as Missy walked up behind him. He headed for a corner of the yard with James in tow.

"He's pretty strong for a half starved dog."

"And he's probably not used to being on a leash." Missy added. "You guys are gonna have to work on that."

Missy stood on the back step and watched

as James followed the dog around the yard. Mac sniffed the perimeter, stopping to lift his leg several times. He finally squatted and dropped a small pile of excrement. Missy laughed when she saw James wrinkle his nose and turn away.

"That reminds me," she said, stifling a giggle. "When you go buy him food, you might want to pick up a pooper-scooper too. Now that he's getting fed on a regular basis, there's going to be a lot more of that to pick up."

"I also have to figure out what to do with him when I'm not home. I can't just let him run around free in the house, but I don't want to lock him in a kennel either."

"Make a bed for him in the laundry room," Missy replied. "You can close him in there if you're only going to be gone for a few hours. If you have to go out of town, I'll stay with him. I'm over here most of the time anyway."

"Thanks. I'd hate to leave him alone or board him somewhere. I don't want him to think he's being abandoned again."

James felt his phone vibrate in his pocket. He pulled it out, read the text message, and bit his lip. He looked up at Missy.

"What are you doing tomorrow?" James slipped the phone back in his pocket. "That was Nestor. I have to head back up to Prescott in the morning. We're finally getting the chance to question Emery Lewis."

Chapter 26

James pulled his car into the parking lot of the sheriff's office. Nestor was getting out of his truck with a cup of coffee in his hand and a notebook tucked under his arm. James parked in the next space over and joined his mentor at the side door.

"How's the dog doing?" Nestor asked, as he swiped his ID card and opened the door. "Is he settling in okay?"

"I think he's going to be all right. I bathed him last night and made him a bed in the laundry room." James pulled the door shut and followed Nestor down the hall. "He whined and howled after I closed him in and went to bed. I felt bad, so I moved his pillow into the bedroom. When I woke up this morning he was curled up on the bed right next to me."

"Dogs are pack animals," Nestor replied. "They sleep together to protect each other. He's accepted you as part of his pack. Just make sure he knows you're the alpha."

"Like you are with Chindi?"

Nestor grinned. "Like Mona is with both of us."

James and Nestor made their way to the conference room, opened up the file boxes, and began reviewing their strategy for questioning

Emery Lewis. James went over the ledger entries again and made some notes while Nestor marked some of the pages in the journals with sticky tabs.

"What time is he supposed to get here?" James asked.

Nestor looked at his watch. "In about half an hour."

"I'm surprised he called you back so soon. I thought it would be harder to convince him to come in and talk to us."

"He didn't call me." Nestor pointed over his shoulder. "I found out he was sitting in the city lockup. He's been there since night before last. They picked him up for DUI and driving on a suspended license. He's being transported here so we can question him."

"He didn't call his wife to get him out?" James paused for a moment. "Or do you think she already knew he'd been arrested and didn't tell us?"

"When I talked to the desk sergeant he said the log didn't show Lewis making any phone calls."

James made a note on his pad. "The way she talked about him yesterday, I get the feeling she wouldn't have bailed him out anyway."

Nestor grinned. "If she did, he probably would have ended up sleeping under the trailer with the dog."

"What happens when he arrives?" James looked at the boxes and files spread out on the table. "Will we be questioning him in here?"

"No, they'll take him to an interview room," Nestor replied. "He's already under arrest, so he'll be treated like any other prisoner. He'll be escorted by an officer, cuffed to the table, and the whole session will be recorded."

James looked up from his notepad. "Audio and video?"

"Yes—and even though we're not arresting him for our crime, we'll still read him his rights and ask him if he wants to talk."

James fumbled with his pen. "What if he asks for a lawyer?"

"Then we pack up, leave the room, and send him back to the city jail until he gets one," Nestor replied. "If we ask him any questions after he says the L-word his answers won't be admissible. That could get the whole interview thrown out if this goes to trial."

"I really hope I don't blow this." James sighed and rubbed his temples. "Especially on video. I'll never hear the end of it from Will."

"You're a smart man—you'll do fine." Nestor's phone pinged and vibrated. He picked it up off the table and checked the message. "Looks like they're here early. You ready for this?"

"Not really." James gathered up a few file folders and his notepad. "I don't think I'll ever be ready, so we might as well get it over with."

"Remember, you're not doing this alone." Nestor patted James on the back as they headed out of the room and down the hall. "We'll handle it just like we talked about yesterday. I'll lead and when you have a question, you speak up."

They rounded a corner and Nestor swiped his ID to get through the locked door. The officer manning the desk on the other side handed Nestor a clipboard and a key.

"Good morning, Deputy Yazzi. Locker seven, and your man is in room four." The officer looked up at James. "You packing?"

James gave Nestor a sideways glance.

"He's not armed."

Nestor signed the log and handed the clipboard back to the officer. He stepped over to a bank of lockers and pulled a concealed gun and an extra magazine out of a holster hidden inside his beltline. He placed both in a locker, closed it, and handed James the key.

"You'd better hold on to this. I've already lost three of them this year."

James slipped the key in his pocket. "If you lose the key, how do you get your gun back?"

"Locksmith." Nestor smiled and pointed James down the hall. "They give you one free pass—it comes out of your paycheck after that."

When they reached the room, a uniformed Prescott PD officer was standing guard. Nestor gave the officer a single nod—without a word, the officer stepped to the side. Nestor put his hand on the knob, paused and took a breath, then opened the door. James saw a gruff looking man in an orange jumpsuit sitting hunched over in the corner. He had one hand cuffed to a steel eyebolt attached to the table and a water bottle clutched in the other. His stringy gray hair hung down past his collar. The man raised his head and groaned.

"You again?" He leaned against the wall. "It's been damn near fifteen years—when the hell are you gonna go away and leave me be?"

"When I solve this case." Nestor took a seat across the table and pulled out a chair for James. "Stray Dog, I'd like you to meet Emery Lewis. Emery, this is Special Investigator James McCarthy."

James reached out to shake Emery's hand. Receiving nothing but an icy stare, he took a seat and said nothing. Nestor set a stack of folders on the table, leaned back, and crossed his arms.

"You want me to read you your rights?" Nestor's face was stone cold and expressionless.

"Why bother? I've heard 'em a hundred times." Emery set the water bottle on the table. "What I want is a drink—a *real* drink."

"Can't help you with that." Nestor opened a folder, pulled out Virgil's last journal and set it on the table. "We'd like to ask you a few questions, if you're up to it."

"Sure, why the hell not. I got nothin' better to do." Emery eyed the journal. "Looks like that book Virg used to scribble in—he leave it behind when he took off?"

"Something like that." Nestor picked up the book and opened it to one of the tabbed pages. "Virgil had some interesting things to say in here about some soil reports."

"What about 'em? We pulled a lot of samples out there. That's how you figure out where to dig."

"Tell me about the samples you took the last few months before Virgil disappeared."

"Hell, I can't remember that far back." Emery rubbed his eyes and pushed the hair out of his face. "I'm lucky if I can remember where I parked my damn truck."

"It's in the city impound yard." Nestor held the book out and pointed to an entry. "Virgil asked you about some samples that didn't look right to him. You remember that?"

"Yeah, we talked a few times. He thought they were a little off, so he wanted to recheck a couple."

Nestor closed the book. "Did he tell you if he ever retested them?"

"That's what he said he was going to do that weekend." Emery took a long swig from the water bottle and wiped his mouth on his sleeve. "He hadn't dug the samples yet when I saw him out there on Saturday."

James spoke up. "What time on Saturday?"

"About eleven." Emery shook his head. "I've answered that question a dozen times."

"I'm sorry. I'm just trying to make sure I get things straight in my head." James scratched a note on his pad. "How long were you with him?"

"Not long," Emery replied. "I was out there maybe half an hour before I headed for Vegas."

James made another note. "You were going to Las Vegas to attend a prospecting show and meet with investors, correct?"

"Yeah, I had a couple of high rollers looking to put some money in." Emery pointed at the file folders on the table and scowled at Nestor. "Has this kid even bothered to read that shit?"

"Every word," Nestor replied, still sporting his best poker face.

Bolstered by Nestor's reply, James sat a

little taller. "What time did you get to your meeting?"

"I don't know." Emery rubbed his neck with his free hand. "I think I checked into the hotel somewhere around four-thirty and took a shower, so it was maybe quarter to six by the time we met up."

"One more question." James flipped back a few pages in his notes. "When we talked to your wife, she said she had to finish some jobs when you weren't . . . um . . . able. Did she ever work out at the mining claim with you?"

"She came out a couple of times to get some paperwork, but that's it."

"Your wife kept the books?" James glanced at Nestor.

"Yeah." Emery rubbed his forehead again. "Me and Virg both sucked at math."

James wrote a few more notes and put his pen down. "Thank you."

"That's it? That's all you hauled me over here for?" Emery growled at Nestor. "You keep digging this shit up and putting some new cop in my face every couple of years. When are you gonna get it through your thick skull? That damn Indian took off and left everybody hanging. Give it up, Yazzi. You've got this kid digging in dry holes and he ain't coming up with nothin' new."

The corners of Nestor's mouth turned up for the first time. "That's where you're wrong."

He opened one of the folders and pulled out a stack of photos. Nestor placed a picture of the half-buried pickup on the table and turned it around toward Emery.

"That's Virgil's truck."

He pulled out another picture, slammed it down on the table, and gritted his teeth.

"And *that's* Virgil!"

Chapter 27

James sat hunched over the conference room table at the sheriff's office and shuffled through his notes and several file folders. He pecked at his laptop, then leaned back in the chair and thought for a moment before hunkering down and scratching some numbers on his notepad. He sat back again and let out a long sigh.

"It doesn't work." He set his pencil down and looked up at Nestor. "It just doesn't work."

"What doesn't work?"

"The timing," James replied. "I've been running the numbers, but the timing doesn't fit."

Nestor set the folder in his hand down. "Talk me through what you've got."

"Emery Lewis said he got out to Virgil at about eleven o'clock and stayed for half an hour." James pointed out a couple of highlighted lines on a sheet of paper. "The credit card records you pulled during the original investigation support his timeline. He stopped at a convenience store on the way out to see Virgil, then got gas in Chino Valley before heading for Las Vegas."

"Okay, so what doesn't work?" Nestor asked.

"I've run the driving time out to where Virgil was and back. Even if he drove as fast as he possibly could on those dirt roads, Lewis couldn't have been out there much more than the thirty minutes he claimed. At the very least, it would have taken a couple of hours to bury the truck—even using the backhoe. And then there's the cleanup of the crime scene. He simply didn't have time to do it."

"He could have killed him in anger and come back later to take care of the scene."

"I ran those numbers, too." James turned his notepad around so Nestor could see. "There was a charge for dinner and drinks just before nine that night, so I'm assuming that was at the end of his meeting with the investors."

"Right." Nestor shrugged. "He could have headed out to the claim after that."

"And do everything he needed to in the dark?" James shook his head. "I don't think so. That level of cleanup had to be done in the daylight. And when you factor in the drive time to get to the area, then be back at the hotel at the time the records show he checked out the next morning, he would have had less than an hour to do everything—and do it in the dark."

"What about Sunday?" Nestor asked. "He could have gone out on his way back from Vegas."

"I checked the times on his charges that day as well. There was another fuel stop in Kingman and a few small purchases in Prescott during the day. When you factor in driving time, there was never a gap big enough to make it out there and back, let alone take care of the body and the evidence."

"So, you're saying you don't think he did it."

"The numbers are saying it," James replied. "Maybe I'm missing something, but I just don't see how it's possible."

"It looks like he had motive and means . . . but no opportunity." Nestor leaned back in his chair. "I guess that puts us back to square one."

"Not exactly square one," James pointed at the stacks on the table. "We've made some pretty good progress. We found Virgil, his diaries, and the coded reports. We have a lot more evidence than we started with."

"But no suspects to go with it." Nestor shook his head and pushed a pile of folders to the side. "All we've managed to do is clear Emery Lewis."

"Let's not eliminate him just yet." James tapped his pencil on the notepad. "He still might factor into the equation somehow."

"I guess he could have fought with him, hit him with the shovel, and then called someone to clean up the mess."

"Or he could have hired someone to take care of Virgil, but that's not likely considering the way he was killed. A hit-man would have brought a weapon." James got up and went to one of the whiteboards. "Maybe we need to look at this from a different perspective."

"Like you did when you created the virtual reality reconstruction of the crime scene?"

"Something like that. You said Lewis had means and motive, but no opportunity." James wrote the three categories across the top of the board. "Anyone could have had the means because the shovel was already at the scene, but they would have needed to know how to run the backhoe to bury the truck."

Nestor gave a nod. "Agreed. That covers means — what about motive?"

"We have the soil samples that could have been tampered with." James made a note. "We also have the money. Virgil discovered a lot of cash being siphoned out of the business."

"True, and that could also point to a disgruntled investor," Nestor replied. "Someone could have gone out there to confront them about the business expenses and no return on their investment."

"Like a loan-shark?" James made another note. "Lewis could have been getting the money from questionable sources."

Nestor cringed. "That could open up a whole new snake pit we don't want to step into. There's a lot of dirty money floating around in those casinos."

James moved to the third column. "Then let's look at opportunity. Who knew where the claim was located?"

"It's a matter of public record." Nestor pointed at James' laptop. "Once they filed the claim, anyone could have looked it up."

"I doubt someone would do that unless they had a specific reason. We should start with a list of everyone who already knew where Virgil was working." James wrote down a few names. "There was Emery and his wife, Virgil's daughter — did her fiancé know where the claim was?"

Nestor nodded. "I think Steve went out there a couple of times to help Virgil."

James added Steve's name to the list. "Is there anyone else you know of?"

Nestor held up his hand. "Me. I was out there several times."

James smiled and raised an eyebrow. "I think we can eliminate you as a suspect. No motive."

Nestor grinned. "I see your sense of humor

is improving. You've nailed sarcasm."

"I'm finding it helps me deal with all of this." James put his hand on a pile of photos sitting on the table. "We've been getting into some pretty dark subject matter."

"Welcome to the world of law enforcement."

"In my case it's temporary. I don't know how you've managed to do this everyday for so many years."

"Strong faith and a good woman," Nestor replied. "Helps to keep you grounded."

"Missy's helped me through a lot of changes, so I think I have the good woman covered. As for the faith . . . I guess we'll have to keep working on that." James went back to the board. "Can you think of anyone else we can put on the list? Maybe they took some of the investors out to the claim."

"We'll have to ask Emery after he gets a lawyer. He may be more willing to talk now that we have evidence to support his alibi." Nestor picked up one of the journals. "Meanwhile, I'll go through these again and see if Virgil mentioned anyone else showing up out there."

"And I'll keep going through the credit card statements and Virgil's paperwork." James paused and held up his finger. "I have a thought."

Nestor smiled. "I like it when you have those. They're usually good ones."

"Earlier, you said that Emery could have killed him and then called someone to take care of things."

"Right."

"What if he called his wife?" James grabbed his notebook and flipped back a couple of pages. "When we talked to her yesterday, Cora Lewis said she had to finish some jobs for Emery when he wasn't able."

"I see where you're going with this," Nestor replied. "You're saying she could have finished this job for him, too."

"And she knows how to use the backhoe." James pointed out an entry in his notebook. "When I climbed up in the seat of the tractor yesterday, it was moved all the way forward. It was clearly set for someone much shorter than Emery."

"Someone about five-foot-three?" Nestor asked?

"I'd say that's just about right." James looked at the piles of papers on the table. "I need to check something."

He shuffled through the folders and found the old pictures from the original investigation. James pulled out the closest shot of the backhoe he could find, inspected the photo and then handed it to Nestor.

"Look at the seat position."

Nestor held the photo up to the light and studied it. The corners of his mouth turned down as he set the photo on the table.

"Emery wasn't the last one to drive that tractor."

Chapter 28

James walked through the front door and set his pack down next to the couch. Before he had a chance to let go of the strap, Mac greeted him with excited yips and a tail wagging so hard it could have stirred up a hurricane. The dog stood on his hind legs and pawed at him. When James bent over to pet him, Mac dropped to the floor and rolled onto his back. He squatted down and rubbed the dog's chest and belly with both hands.

"I thought I closed you in the laundry room this morning." Mac flipped back over and sat up. James put his arms around him and hugged. "You're just full of surprises. Did you figure out how to open the door?"

"I let him out." Missy stepped out of the kitchen. "I didn't have any clients at the salon this afternoon, so I came over early to see how he was doing. I felt kind of sorry for the little guy. It's his first time being stuck here all alone in a strange place."

"I was a little worried about that too." James stood and reached for the leash hanging on the coat hook by the door. "I guess I should take him for a walk so he can do his business."

"He already took care of that," Missy replied.

James looked down at Mac and wrinkled his forehead. "Did he do it in the house?"

"Nope." Missy hugged her boyfriend and gave him a kiss. "When I came in, he was dancing around at the back door, so I let him out in the yard."

"He's already house broken?" James bent down to pet Mac. "That's a good boy."

Missy giggled. "You won't think it's so good when you have to clean it up. He's still adjusting to the dog food. Things are going to be a little messy for a while."

"Things are a little messy up north too," James replied. "The case isn't turning out the way I thought it would."

James sat on the couch and Missy joined him. Mac put his head on the cushion next to her and looked up with his big, brown eyes. She smiled and sighed.

"Come on." Missy patted her leg. Mac jumped into her lap, laid down, and rested his head on James' knee. "He's been doing this every time I sit down. I just can't say no."

"He does it to me too," James rubbed Mac behind the ears. "He slept on my bed last night."

"I'm not surprised. You're a soft touch and he seems pretty smart. I'm sure he's already getting you trained." Missy turned her attention back to James. "So, what happened up there today? I'm guessing that Lewis guy didn't confess."

James shook his head. "No, he didn't. In fact, he looked totally shocked when Nestor showed him the picture of Virgil's remains. I don't know if it was because he didn't know Virgil was dead, or he was surprised we were able to find the body. Either way, he asked for a lawyer, so we had to end the interview."

"It would be nice to have a confession, but you don't really need it, right? You'll find a way to prove he did it."

"I'm not so sure. I ran the numbers and he was never unaccounted for long enough to have committed the murder and taken care of burying the evidence." James unconsciously stroked the dog's soft fur. "If he killed Virgil, someone else did the cleanup."

"Well, if he didn't kill him, who did?"

"We started making a list of possible suspects, but there's already one who stands out—Cora Lewis, Emery's wife."

"His wife?" Missy turned her head and arched her eyebrows. "What makes you think she might've done it?"

"Motive, means, and opportunity," James replied. "That's what Nestor said we need to look for. She has a couple of motives. Mrs. Lewis kept the books, so she had to know about the money issues."

"Or she could have been the one causing them," Missy added. "If she had control of the books, then she probably had control of the bank account too."

"True. Emery may not have even known about the missing funds, but I don't think that's very likely."

"What other motive did she have?" Missy asked.

"Virgil went out that weekend to retake some samples and double check some of Emery's results," James replied. "She may have gone out there to talk to him and things got out of hand."

"Okay, so what about means?" Missy asked. "The shovel was already there, so all it needed was somebody pissed off enough to swing it. That could be anybody."

"Yes, but means also includes the ability to take care of the evidence. Cora Lewis had that as well. She knew how to run the backhoe."

"A lot of people know how to run a backhoe," Missy replied. "I could probably figure it out if I had to."

James smiled. "I'm sure you could, if given enough time, but the job had to be done fast.

Whoever buried the truck already knew how to use the equipment."

"What makes you think it might have been her?"

"In the photos of the tractor, the seat was too far forward for Emery — but it was set to the right position for Cora's height."

Missy nodded. "That just leaves opportunity."

"I'm afraid that one's wide open," James sighed. "We have no way of knowing where she was the day Virgil was killed. No evidence was ever collected from her back then because she wasn't a suspect. It's been so long, I doubt we could find anything now."

"How did you figure out Emery Lewis didn't have the time?"

"His credit card records were in the old files," James replied. "We built a timeline based on when and where he charged things like gas and food."

Missy thought for a moment. "Was his wife's credit card tied to the same account? If it was, then shouldn't her charges be on the same bills?"

"I'll check when I go back on Monday, but it's possible she didn't charge anything that weekend. She wasn't traveling like Emery."

"So there may not be any charges to prove where she was."

"Or where she wasn't," James replied. "The card statements actually supported Emery's alibi and showed he couldn't have killed Virgil—at least not without someone else to take care of the evidence for him."

"What about phone records?" Missy asked. "If Lewis called his wife to help, maybe there's a record of the call."

"I doubt the phone company keeps records that far back, but it's worth asking," James rubbed the back of his neck. "It would also mean having to get a warrant and we'd have to show probable cause to get a judge to sign off on it."

Missy rolled her eyes. "You're starting to sound like a real cop."

"Between working with Nestor, and the things Will's had me do, I'm starting to feel like one," James sighed.

Missy laid her head on his shoulder. "You worry me sometimes. Please tell me you're not thinking about changing careers."

James smiled and shook his head. "I could never see myself carrying a gun around and chasing criminals, but I have to admit I like the challenge this investigation has presented. It's working my brain in a whole new way."

"If there's one thing your brain doesn't need, it's more exercise. You need to learn how to relax."

"Maybe this little guy will help me with that." James ran his hand down the dog's back. "What do you think, Mac? Should we head over to the pub and introduce you to the rest of the family?"

"He's got an appointment with the vet first." Missy got up, grabbed the leash, and handed it to James. "We'll stop at the pet supply store afterward and get you that pooper-scooper."

Chapter 29

Nestor stepped into the interview room at the sheriff's office. Emery Lewis raised his head and took off his cap. He pushed his greasy hair back and set the hat on the table. Nestor took a seat across from Lewis, dropped a folder in front of him, and crossed his arms.

"Where's your lawyer?"

"Don't have one," Lewis replied in a monotone. "Where's your sidekick?"

"Phoenix." Nestor barely moved a muscle in his face as he spoke. "You want to talk without a lawyer?"

Lewis nodded. "Yup."

"This is on the record." Nestor tilted his head toward the camera in the upper corner of the room. "Do you want me to read you your rights?"

"I know my damn rights. Just you, me, and the truth, Yazzi. No lawyers, no holds barred."

Nestor gave a single nod. "No jumpsuit today either. Cora bail you out?"

"She's not pickin' up the phone," Lewis harrumphed. "Judge cut me loose until my court date."

"All right." Nestor uncrossed his arms and rested his hands on the table. "You called me. What do you want to talk about?"

"I want to talk about Virgil." Lewis lowered his head. "That picture you showed me . . . that really him? Is Virg really dead?"

"It's him. Dental records confirmed it."

Emery leaned back in his chair and stared at the ceiling. He rubbed his eyes and then pushed the hair out of his face before making eye contact with Nestor.

"He was pissed about some assay results—thought I might be trying to pull one over on him. I figured he got himself in a snit and took off. Where'd you find him?"

Nestor shook his head. "Open investigation—can't give you any details."

"Can you at least tell me if he suffered?"

"Never knew what hit him," Nestor replied, stone-faced.

Emery turned away and wiped his eyes with the cuff of his flannel shirt. He sniffed a couple of times, took a deep breath, and then cleared his throat. "I know you've got a pretty low opinion of me, but Virgil was a friend—I never could've hurt him."

Nestor leaned forward. "Then who did?"

"Hell, I don't know. When he went missing, I was in Vegas trying to scrape up enough money to keep us working." Emery sniffed again and swallowed hard. "I knew we were getting close to something, but we were running low on cash."

"Where did all of the money go?"

Emery shrugged. "The backhoe, fuel, soil testing . . . stuff like that."

"What about travel?" Nestor asked. "You spent a lot on hotels and entertainment."

"Sure, I dropped some bucks when I was working investors, but I stayed at the cheapest hotels I could find — sometimes I slept in my truck."

"And the big cash withdrawals? What was that money for?"

"What are you talking about?" Emery sneered. "The only time I took a big chunk was when we bought the backhoe . . . and Virg was with me."

Nestor leaned back and rubbed his chin. "You're telling me you weren't making withdrawals on a regular basis? How did you get reimbursed for expenses?"

"I'd give the receipts to my old lady and she'd handle it — Virg did the same thing. Like I said before, neither one of us was any good at numbers, so Cora handled the books for us."

Nestor thought for a moment. "Did she handle the soil samples too?"

"Nah, that was usually me and Virg," Emery replied. "She may have dropped a few off at the lab for me, but that's it."

"Were any of the samples she took for you the ones Virgil questioned?"

"I don't know . . . maybe." Emery shifted in his seat and fiddled with his hat. "I was going out of town a lot to raise money the last few months before Virgil disappeared. She might have dropped off more samples for me than she usually did."

"I'm going to ask you something and I want an honest answer." Nestor opened the folder and pulled out one of the assay reports. "Did you salt any of these samples?"

"What?" Emery sat straight up. "Why the hell would I do something like that?"

"To make things look better to the investors," Nestor replied. "Or maybe to keep Virgil putting every last dime he could scrape up into the operation so you could take it out."

"That's bullshit!" Emery narrowed his eyes and clenched his jaw. "When Virg said he was gonna retest those holes, I told him to go for it. And another thing—where the hell would I get the material to mix in? If I had a place to get good samples, we'd of been digging there instead."

"Then how do you explain this?" Nestor set another report next to the first one. "This is a sample Virgil took in the same location. It shows only trace amounts — the one you took looks like you could pay the rent with one shovel full."

Emery picked up the reports, looked each one over, and then laid them on the table side-by-side. He ran a finger down each page, stopping to compare every line. When he reached the bottoms of the pages, he sat back and shook his head.

"I don't get it. I mean I could've hit a washout pocket or something, but this is way off." Emery leaned back down again and looked at the top of the first report. "Hold on a minute. I didn't fill out the paperwork on this sample."

Nestor inspected the paper. "Your name is at the top."

"I'm telling you I didn't submit this." Emery pointed at the name of the submitter. "I never use my middle initial."

"You think this is one of the samples your wife dropped off?"

"Could be. She usually puts her middle initial in when she fills something out."

Nestor pulled out a few more of the questionable reports and checked the names. He set them on the table facing Emery.

"Middle initials — the whole lot."

Emery's eyes widened as looked up at Nestor. "You're not thinking—"

"—that Cora could have spiked the

samples?" Nestor nodded. "If you didn't do it, who else is left?"

"Why?" Emery slumped back in his chair. "Why the hell would she do something like that?"

Nestor shrugged. "My guess? To keep the money coming in. As long as things looked promising, Virgil would keep digging and you'd keep rounding up cash."

"Son-of-a—" Emery bit his lip. "You think I killed Virgil and threw him over a cliff somewhere to cover this up?"

"No, I don't," Nestor replied. "Stray Dog— Mr. McCarthy—already proved you couldn't have done it—not alone, anyway."

Emery crossed his arms and glared at Nestor. "You can't pin this on me, so you're dragging my family into it?"

"We're just following the evidence. Can you think of anyone else who would have done this? Disgruntled investor? Another prospector? Who else knew where you were working?"

Emery shook his head. "We never told anybody where we were digging, not even the people we were getting money from. That's the number one rule when you're prospecting—keep a tight lip. Only ones who knew exactly where we were working were family and close friends we knew we could trust."

"If you didn't know the samples were salted, why'd you stop digging out there after Virgil disappeared?" Nestor put a hand on the pile of reports. "You had some good results, or so you thought."

"No money left and it didn't feel right without Virg, so I packed up the gear and tried to make a living with the backhoe."

"And you just abandoned the operation? I'm sure your investors weren't too happy about that."

Emery shook his head. "No, they weren't. I offered to sign over the claim to a couple of them, but they didn't want it. They cut their losses and moved on."

Nestor collected the reports, returned them to the folder, and pulled out a copy of the spreadsheet James made from the coded ledger.

"Let's talk about the money." Nestor laid out the spreadsheet. "I see a lot of questionable entries in here."

Emery looked at the papers on the table. "Where did this come from?"

"When Virgil didn't like what he was seeing, he started tracking things himself."

"I don't know where he was getting his information, but some of this stuff is dead wrong." Emery pointed out a couple of lines. "I never spent that much on a hotel room in my life. That's almost a month's rent!"

"Credit card statements showed some of those reimbursements were triple what the actual charges were." Nestor put the sheet back in the folder with the rest of the paperwork. "Virgil must have got access to the books somehow and copied the entries. Did Cora ever have the books out when he was around?"

"Couple of times, maybe." Emery rubbed his face and wrinkled his forehead, "Come to think of it, there was one time she couldn't find the ledger book. It turned up a day or two later in the bottom of a drawer. She swore she didn't put it there. That was maybe a week before Virg went missing."

"Had Virgil been to the house around that time?"

"Yeah, that's when he told me he was going out to pull the new samples. Come to think of it, Cora heard us talking about it. She didn't like the idea of spending the extra money to retest." Emery stood up and grabbed his hat. "I think it's high time I had a serious talk with that woman!"

Nestor got up, stepped in front of the door, and crossed his arms.

"Not before I do."

Chapter 30

Mac lay curled up on the passenger seat as James made the drive from Phoenix to Prescott. He kept one hand on the dog while he thought through every detail of the case. He played out several scenarios in his mind, putting himself in the shoes of both the killer and the victim. As the miles rolled by, he contemplated the evidence from every possible angle. By the time he pulled into the parking lot of the sheriff's office, he'd watched no less than two dozen different versions play out like movies projected on the windshield of the car.

James grabbed his bag out of the back seat and led Mac to the side door. He swiped his ID badge and made his way to the conference room where Nestor was already sipping coffee and shuffling through papers. Mac yipped, wagged his tail, and pulled James around to Nestor's side of the table.

"Good morning." Nestor smiled and scratched the excited dog behind the ears. "Is it bring your pet to work day? I must have missed that memo."

"He looked so sad when I was getting dressed this morning," James replied. "I just couldn't leave him. I hope it was okay to bring him with me."

Nestor nodded. "I don't have a problem with it, but you might want to close the door so he doesn't go exploring."

"Thanks for understanding." James let go of the leash, closed the conference room door, and unpacked his laptop. "How was your weekend?"

"My weekend was very enlightening. I had a visitor." Nestor picked up a DVD, slipped it out of its plastic sleeve, and handed it to James. "You should take a look at this."

"Home movies?" James sat down and popped the disk into his computer. "Did your granddaughters come to visit?"

Nestor shook his head. "Nope, Emery Lewis showed up—without a lawyer."

"No lawyer?" James' eyes locked onto the screen as the video started to play. "I thought we weren't allowed to question him after he asked for one."

"He changed his mind and waived his rights." Nestor pointed at the laptop. "Watch the whole interview and then we'll talk about it."

James turned up the sound and stayed glued to the screen. He hit the keyboard several times stopping the video to replay a section, getting closer to the laptop and squinting. As Carl had suggested, James paid close attention to Emery Lewis' eyes and body language. When the video finished, he ejected the disk and handed it back to Nestor.

"Well, what do you think?" Nestor leaned back in his chair. "Give me your gut reaction."

James closed his laptop and crossed his hands on top of it. "My first impression is that he's telling the truth—he didn't kill Virgil. He looked pretty upset when you confirmed Virgil was really dead. I didn't see anything to make me think he was faking it."

Nestor sighed. "I agree. The man I talked to in that room was broken. For fourteen years he thought he'd been betrayed by a friend. By the end of that interview, he knew he'd been lied to by his wife."

"Have you questioned her again?"

"Not yet." Nestor rested his hand on a pile of folders. "I want to look into a few things before we bring her in."

"I hope Emery didn't confront her when he got home." James replied. "If she knows we found Virgil, that could mess things up for us when we question her, right?"

"It could, but it won't." A narrow smile came across Nestor's face. "He hasn't talked to her, or been back to Wilhoit since he got picked up on the DUI charge. He called me as soon as the judge cut him loose." Nestor put the DVD back in its sleeve and set it aside. "After the interview, he agreed to go back to my place for a couple of days. Mona's making sure he stays sober and quiet until we can talk to Cora."

James stiffened up. "I'm pretty sure he didn't kill Virgil, but do you really think it's safe to leave him alone with your wife?"

Nestor grinned, showing some teeth this time. "As long as he doesn't get out of line, I don't think she'll hurt him."

James relaxed a little and shook his head. "When you say things like that, I'm never sure if you're serious or just kidding."

"The best jokes always have a kernel of truth at their core. That's what makes them funny." Nestor smiled and went back to work. "I wouldn't worry about Mona. What she can't handle, Chindi can."

"I wouldn't mess with either one of them," James mumbled. He shuffled through one of the boxes stacked up next to the table and pulled out a file folder. "I'm beginning to think it's not a good idea to mess with Cora Lewis either."

"We're in agreement on that. Now the question is, can we put her at the scene?" Nestor pulled out a photo of the backhoe. "The seat position on the tractor isn't exactly a smoking gun, but it will shore up a circumstantial case if we can build one."

"I was talking to Missy over the weekend and she had an idea." James opened the folder in his hand and laid a stack of papers on the table. "We used these credit card records to figure out where Emery was that weekend. If her card was tied to the same account, maybe we can get an idea of her movements as well."

"It's worth a shot." Nestor reached across the table and picked up a few of the pages. "At the very least, maybe we can find some leverage to loosen her tongue and get her talking."

James took one of the remaining pages and ran his finger down the list of charges. "There was a second card active on the account. I see several transactions here."

"Let's concentrate on the charges from that weekend." Nestor shuffled through his pages. "We already have Emery's purchases for that time period highlighted, so everything else should be Cora's."

"I think I have the page for that weekend." James pulled another sheet from the stack and read down the list. "The second card only shows one charge on Saturday. She bought gas in Prescott at eight-thirty that morning. At least that tells us she was in the general area the day Virgil went missing."

"Not much help," Nestor replied. "They were living in town back then. Anything on Sunday?"

James shook his head. "Just Emery's transactions." He scanned the next page. "Here's something interesting on Monday. It's a cash draw against the second card from an ATM."

Nestor shrugged. "What's so interesting about it?"

"The location." James held up the paper and pointed out the entry. "This machine is inside the casino on the hill north of town."

Nestor's eyebrows peaked. "How do you know?"

"Missy and I got cash there one weekend," James replied. "That's exactly how it showed up on my card statement."

Nestor looked down the list of charges on the sheets in his hand. "I see several cash draws at the same place."

"I've got more as well." James highlighted a few lines. "She was taking a lot of cash advances on that card and most of them were at the casino."

"So, Cora might've had a gambling problem." Nestor set the papers down. "That could explain why they dumped the house and ended up in that trailer less than a year after the investors bailed."

"It also gives her a stronger motive. If Virgil was getting close to the truth, it could have cost Cora her marriage, and probably her freedom."

"One more piece of the puzzle." Nestor picked up another page. "Let's keep digging."

"What about her phone records?" James asked. "Can we track her that way?"

Nestor shook his head. "Depending on the carrier, they only hold that information for eighteen months to seven years."

James thought for a moment. "What about her job? If she needed money she might have been stealing from there as well. If there were any unsolved thefts reported by her employer at that time, maybe we can link those to her. That might give us probable cause to dig deeper into her finances."

"It could help establish a pattern of behavior, but we wouldn't be able to get a warrant to pull her bank records based on the information. The Statute of Limitations on something like that would have expired years ago."

James scanned the card statements again. Another one of the entries caught his eye.

"I don't know how I missed this the first time." He highlighted another charge and handed the paper to Nestor. "She bought gas on Saturday evening too."

"She filled up twice in one day?" Nestor looked over the charge. "Figuring for the price of gas at the time, I'd say she got a little more than nine gallons — and that station is in Chino Valley."

"It's near where we left the main highway to get out to Virgil's campsite," James replied. "And that's a little more fuel than we used to get out there and back."

"Pull together everything we have on Cora Lewis and get it organized." Nestor picked up his cell phone. "I'll send a unit out to Wilhoit to pick her up."

Chapter 31

James pecked away at his laptop, organizing information and formulating the questions he wanted to ask Cora Lewis. Mac snored while napping under the table, his head resting on James' foot. Nestor sat on the other side of the conference table with his cell phone pressed to his ear and the corners of his mouth downturned. After shaking his head and mumbling a few inaudible words, he ended the call and tossed the phone on the note pad in front of him.

"Cora's not at the trailer," he growled. "The neighbors told the officers they saw her pull out day before yesterday and she hasn't been back since."

James stopped typing and looked up from his computer. "Do you think Emery warned her? He could have lied about not being able to reach her."

Nestor shook his head. "No calls from jail went through and his cell phone is still in his truck down at the city impound yard. More likely she got spooked and bolted after we questioned her."

"How are we going to find her now?" James asked. "With a two day head start she could be just about anywhere."

"I doubt she's gone too far," Nestor

drummed on the table with his fingers. "She's driving a thirty year old car that's falling apart and she has very little money."

"Does she still have a credit card?" James put his hand on the pile of old card statements. "If we can get access to her current records, maybe we can find her that way."

"By the time we get a warrant and access to the account, it'll be old information." Nestor stood up, picked up his phone and coat, and motioned to James. "Grab your stuff. I know a faster way to get into those records."

James closed his laptop and slipped it into his pack. "Where are we going?"

"To my house," Nestor replied. "If Emery's on the account, he can get us in."

"Do you think he'll cooperate? We'll be asking him to help catch his own wife."

"I don't think that will be a problem." Nestor headed for the door. "He was pretty hot last night—complained about her all the way through dinner and didn't shut up until he went to bed."

Mac led the way as the two men headed down the hall, out of the station, and into Nestor's truck. The drive to his house took only minutes. Nestor was the first one out of the vehicle and up to the front door. Chindi greeted the pair in his usual, boisterous manner, dancing around Nestor as they made their way into the house. He stopped and let out a low growl when he spotted Mac. Mac lowered his head, tucked his tail, and hid behind James.

Nestor snapped his fingers, pointed, and shook his head. Chindi backed off and sat, letting the new dog enter.

Emery was sitting on the couch with a cup of coffee in one hand and the TV remote in the other. He turned off the TV and stood up as Mona emerged from the kitchen.

"Should'a told me you were coming home for lunch," she grumbled. "Didn't make enough for everybody."

Nestor held up his hand. "Not here for lunch. We're here to talk to Emery."

"You're here, might as well eat." Mona turned back toward the kitchen. "You talk—I'll throw together a couple of sandwiches."

Nestor took a seat in his recliner. James and Emery settled on opposite ends of the couch. Mac sat on the floor next to James and leaned heavy on his leg. Emery stared at the dog, and then at James.

"Ain't that the mutt that's living under my trailer?"

"Yes." James smiled and rubbed Mac's head. "I adopted him."

"Glad somebody got him before the old lady called the dog catcher. I've been slipping him food when she's not looking."

James smiled. "I guess that's why he stuck around."

"Guess so." Emery turned to Nestor. "That's one tough old bird you got in there." He stared in the direction of the kitchen. "Couldn't find my clothes when I got up this morning. She had 'em in the washer. Threw me a robe and told me to get in the shower and don't come out until I don't stink anymore."

"She's tough, but she's honest," Nestor replied.

"And that damn dog." Emery shook his finger at Chindi. "Growls like a demon every time I get near the front door."

"He's doing his job." Nestor put a hand on Chindi and rubbed him behind the ears, then locked eyes with Emery. "Got some news. Cora's gone."

"Gone?" Emery leaned forward. "Whadda ya mean gone?"

"According to the neighbors, she took off a couple days ago," Nestor replied. "Looks like she left you swinging in the breeze."

Emery balled his fists and jumped up off the couch. Chindi let out a low, deep growl and bared his teeth slightly. Emery froze, then slowly lowered himself back to his seat. He swallowed hard and spoke without taking his eyes off the massive beast.

"Where the hell did she go?"

Nestor shrugged. "I don't have any idea."

"We were hoping you could help us find her," James interjected. "Does she have a credit card we can track?"

"We haven't been able to get one for years, but she has one of these." Emery pulled out his wallet and took out a card. "It's one of those prepaid cards—you know, you go to the check cashing place and load it up so you can use it when you gotta have plastic."

James took the card and looked it over. "There's a website where you can check the balance. We might be able to get purchase history there as well. You don't happen to have her card number, do you?"

"Nope. Don't even have mine memorized."

"Do you think she has a record of it at home?" James asked.

Emery shook his head. "I doubt it. That woman doesn't trust a soul—even me. What she doesn't shred, she keeps in one of them expanding files. If she took off for good, there's no way she'd leave without it."

James handed the card back to Emery and turned to Nestor. "What do we do now?"

"When an animal's scared or wounded, it heads for somewhere familiar." Nestor sat forward in his chair and stared into Emery's eyes. "Where would Cora run to? Where does she feel safe?"

Emery hung his head and rubbed the back of his neck with his rough hand. "I don't know. She could be anywhere by now."

"Not with that old car of hers and no money." Nestor tapped the top of the coffee table with his fingertip. "It'll be somewhere close to home. She'll find a hole to crawl into until she figures out her next move. You know of anyplace like that?"

"She's got a sister in Wickenburg," Emery replied. "She might head there."

"I doubt it." James frowned. "Too obvious. If she was smart enough to cover her tracks for fourteen years, she has to know that's the first place we'll look."

"I agree, but we'll send a unit out there anyway to be sure." Nestor pulled out his phone. "Got a name and address?"

"Tallulah Morgan—goes by Tally. I don't know the address, but she lives off Vulture Mine Road south of the highway," Emery replied. "Should be easy to find. I doubt there's more than one Tallulah in a town that size."

Nestor made a quick call and then stowed his phone.

"Anyplace else you can think of?"

Emery shrugged. "Not off the top of my head."

"What about friends?" James pulled his notepad out of his pack. "We know she used to go to the casino. Did she ever talk about people she met there?"

"You know about that, huh?" Emery grumbled. "Guess you guys know just about everything by now."

"Not everything," Nestor replied. "That's why we need your help. Think hard. Who does she hang out with?"

"In the last few years? Nobody." Emery leaned back on the couch and stared at the pictures on the walls. "Back when she was gambling, there were a couple of regulars that came around— poker players. She got in pretty deep to one of 'em."

"Is that when you lost the house?" Nestor asked.

"Yeah." Emery hung his head. "Had to sell it to settle a loan she took out without telling me."

James scratched something on his pad. "Is that when you moved to Wilhoit?"

"Not right away. Couldn't even afford to rent a cardboard box at that point. One of her poker buddies let us use his weekend place while I did some tractor work on the property and picked some odd jobs around town to get a little money together."

Nestor slid forward on his chair. "How far away is that property?"

"Maybe forty minutes," Emery replied. "It's in a small canyon on the east side of Mingus Mountain."

The corners of Nestor's mouth turned up. "Grab your coat, Emery. We're going for a ride."

Chapter 32

James sat in the back seat of Nestor's truck with Mac by his side. The dog stayed pressed tight up against him as Nestor turned off the pavement onto a dirt road. The freshly graded earthen strip split the landscape in two, with a grassy prairie to the right and Mingus Mountain rising gently on the left. They came to a barbed wire fence and Emery jumped out of the truck to open the gate. When he climbed back into the cab, Mac leapt to his feet, stuck his head between the front seats, and barked.

"Why'd you have to bring that mutt?" Emery growled.

"Chindi didn't look too happy when I brought him in the house." James pulled the dog up against him again. "I didn't think it was a good idea to leave him there."

Emery half grinned. "That monster wasn't too happy about me being in the house either."

"No reason for you to stay there now," Nestor replied. "I'm sure Cora's already figured out we're onto her."

"Not much reason to go home either." Emery hung his head. "Can't believe she's been lying to me all these years—letting everybody think I did something to Virg. If I knew what she'd done, I'd have turned her ass in a long time ago."

"And I wouldn't blame you. Let's hope we find her." Nestor pointed up the road in front of them. "How much farther?"

"We're on public land now." Emery replied. "There's another gate about two miles south. Once we go through, we're back on private property. We'll pass a cabin, then make a left and head up into a canyon."

As they dropped into a wash, James tried to pull up a satellite map on his phone, but nothing loaded.

"I'm not getting a good cell signal."

"Yeah, the coverage out here sucks." Emery pointed up the mountain. "You can pick it up on the high ground in a few spots, but once we turn into that canyon, you're screwed until we come back out."

James slipped his phone back in his pocket. "At least we know no one can call your wife to warn her we might be coming,"

"If she's even there." Nestor looked around and chewed his bottom lip as they passed a small herd of cattle. "This area looks familiar."

"Looks like every other damn place out here if you ask me." Emery adjusted the bill of his hat to block the mid-day sun. "You've been around here a long time, Yazzi. I'll bet you've covered every inch of this county at one time or another."

Nestor gazed up the slope. "Maybe, but there's something about this place . . . something familiar."

"When we were staying out here, I made this drive every day for a couple of months pulling that tractor," Emery snorted. "I'm familiar with every damn inch if it."

James leaned forward and spoke up. "You said you were doing some excavating for the owner, right? What did he have you working on?"

"I was leveling part of the lot, and digging the basement and footings for the main house."

"The main house?" James asked. "So there's more than one house on the property?"

Emery shook his head. "There was a garage and a fifth-wheel trailer—that's where we stayed. They didn't build the house until the power and septic system were in."

Nestor continued scanning the area. "I know I've been out here before." He took a hand off the wheel and rubbed the back of neck. "Whose place did you say this was?"

"Some poker buddy of Cora's. I never met the guy face to face," Emery replied. "His contractor came out a couple of times to show me where he needed the work done and to check up on it. I only talked to the owner on the phone once or twice. Cora dealt with him most of the time."

Nestor pulled up to the second gate and stopped. Emery got out again and pushed it open, waited for the truck to pass, then closed it and hopped back in.

"Make a left about 200 yards up." Emery waved with the back of his hand. "Just past that cabin on the left."

Not long after Nestor made the turn, the dry golden grass of the plain disappeared, giving way to heavy brush. As the road snaked up the narrow canyon, the temperature began to drop. Junipers and pinion pines took over the landscape. A mile or so up the mountain, the canyon opened up and flattened out a little. They passed through another gate and pulled into a clearing. A two story cabin sat just outside the tree line. A breezeway connected the large, open garage to the house. Nestor parked in front of the house, rolled down his window, and shut the truck off. He eyed the structures before opening his door and stepping out.

"Stay in the truck." Nestor closed his door. "I don't see any cars, but that doesn't mean no one's here."

Nestor walked around the front of the truck and approached the door. He rested his right hand on the butt of the gun in his holster and peered around the side of the garage. Stepping up onto on the porch, he tried to look in the front window, but the curtains were drawn. Nestor knocked on the door and stepped back. Receiving no answer he knocked louder and tried the doorknob—locked. Returning to the truck, he leaned in the window.

"No one's answering the door." Nestor pointed at the peak of the roof. "But there's a little smoke coming out of the chimney. Somebody's either in that house or left just before we got here."

James turned and looked back toward the gate. "We didn't pass anyone on our way in."

"If you keep going south on that main road, it comes back out on Highway 69 just north of Dewey," Emery replied. "If we head out that way, we might catch up to her before she hits the blacktop."

Nestor shook his head. "We'd just be chasing our tails. We don't even know if Cora's been here."

Mac's ears perked up. He jumped to his feet and barked in Nestor's direction. James grabbed the dog's collar and pulled him back.

"Stop it! Why are you barking at Nestor?"

"He wasn't looking at me, he was looking at those trees." Nestor reached through the window and patted Mac's head. "What'd you see, boy? Is there something back there?"

"Probably an antelope or a deer," Emery grumbled. "The place is thick with 'em."

"He saw something. It's worth taking a look." Nestor motioned to James. "Come on, Stray Dog—and bring the pup."

When James opened his door, Mac jumped over him and onto the ground, pulling him out of the truck by his leash. Emery got out as well and came around the back of the vehicle. Nestor pointed toward the tree line where the dog had alerted.

"What's back there?"

"Not much," Emery replied. "The property goes up another fifty yards before you get to the fence. You're on National Forest beyond that."

Nestor nodded and motioned for everyone to follow as he headed for the trees. When they passed the side of the garage, Emery stopped and whistled to get Nestor's attention. He pointed at a tarp-covered car parked behind the building. One corner of the tarp was folded back, like the wind had blown it off, exposing a light blue two-door sedan.

"Cora's?" Nestor asked.

Emery shook his head. "Her sister's"

"Why would her sister's car be here?" James asked, holding the dog back. "Does she know the property owner too?"

"Not that I ever heard of," Emery replied. "Maybe that junker of Cora's gave up the ghost, so she grabbed Tally's car."

James looked confused. "But if she made it all the way down to Wickenburg, why would she turn around and come back up here? She could have kept going and been out of the state by now."

"She must have come back for something," Nestor replied. "Has she ever hidden anything here before, Emery?"

"Damned if I know." Emery leaned on side the of the building and crossed his arms. "Looks like she's been hiding a lot from me."

Nestor pulled a small notepad from his shirt pocket and wrote down the license number. He turned back toward the trees and pointed at the ground. "Fresh tracks."

Emery walked past Nestor, squatted down, and inspected the marks. "Those look like Cora's boot prints. Size and tread pattern are right."

Mac pulled hard on the leash, jerking James in the direction of the tree line again. James dug his heels in and pulled back.

"He really wants to go."

"He's a smart dog. Let's see where he leads us." Nestor turned to Emery. "You hang back here and stay out of sight. If she doubles back, give me a whistle and try to keep her here."

Emery nodded and slipped around the corner of the garage.

"And you keep your head down, Stray Dog. We don't know if she's armed." Nestor reached down and rubbed Mac's head. "Alright boy, show us what you saw."

Chapter 33

Mac darted from side to side sniffing the ground and dragging James along behind him. Nestor followed the pair as they made their way through the trees. When the group reached a barbed wire fence at the back of the property, the dog stuck his head through and pushed on the wire.

"Hold on, Mac." James pulled back on the leash, stopping him before he could impale himself on a barb, and then turned to Nestor. "What do we do now?"

"We hop the fence and keep going. Your dog's on a hot trail."

"How do we know he's following Cora Lewis and not some animal?"

"We don't, but I like the odds. Her tracks were headed this way before we lost them, and he knows her scent from living under her trailer."

"But she was mean to him," James replied. "Why would he want to follow her instead of running away?"

"Emery slipped him food every now and then. He may still associate the smells from that place with getting fed."

James held the dog back. "I guess that makes sense."

Nestor stepped up to the fence and put his

foot on the middle wire, pushing it down as far as he could. He grabbed the top strand and stretched it upward, then motioned for James to climb through the gap. As soon as he stepped forward slacking the leash, Mac jumped through the opening, nearly pulling him into the sharp points on the wire. He regained control just in time, and then ducked sideways through the opening. James turned and held the wires in the same manner, allowing Nestor to pass through. When he turned loose of the fence, Mac surged forward again leading James to a spot on the fence-line about fifteen feet up the hill.

"It looks like this is where she came through." James pointed at the loose soil. "Those are the same boot prints we saw before."

Nestor pulled a couple of blue threads off of a barb and held them up. "We're on the right track." He turned and looked up through the trees. "She could be heading for that ridge. The high ground would give her an advantage. She probably knows we're coming."

"She may also be going up there to get a cell signal." James held the dog back as he sniffed the ground, locked onto the scent again, and pulled on the leash. "That's the direction Mac wants to go."

"Follow his lead. He's kept us on her trail so far."

James gave a quick nod and the group took off again. Mac headed up the hill following the trail of prints. As the terrain pitched up, the path crossed back and forth across the mountain in a serpentine pattern. James did his best to keep his footing while Mac continued to pull him up the hill. Nestor followed at a steady pace, his footfalls as stable as a mountain goat. When they crested the top of the ridge, James heard a pinging sound and his phone vibrated.

"Email—that means I've got a cell signal." He pulled the phone out of his pocket. "I think we can assume Cora has it too."

Nestor dipped his chin in agreement. "She may have called someone for help—most likely whoever owns that cabin she's hiding in."

James started typing on his phone. "I'll see if I can find out who the property owner is."

"Later." Nestor pointed at the boot prints heading down the ridgeline. "We need to keep moving."

James poked at his phone for a few more seconds before stuffing it back in his pocket. "I texted Will our location. Maybe he can research the property and get back to us." He stepped forward, slacking the leash again. "Come on, Mac. Let's go."

The dog surged forward. He continued down the ridge for a short distance before making a sharp turn and leading the men down the other side of the hill. Nestor paid close attention to the details of Cora's footprints whenever they were visible.

"Her steps are farther apart and striking the ground harder." He pointed at a series of prints in a sandy area near the bottom of the hill. "Looks like she's running."

James stretched out his gait. "Then we'd better speed up."

Nestor reached out and caught him by the back of the jacket. "If we rush we could miss something or lose the trail. Just keep moving steady. Cora's not a young woman. She can't hold that pace for too long before she'll have to catch her breath."

Mac continued to lead James and Nestor into the next valley. When the tracks brought them to another fence, they crossed it in the same manner as the first and made their way into a clearing. James saw a weathered wooden shed in the middle of a dry, grassy area, but no cabin. He pulled back on Mac's leash.

"It looks like we're back on private property. Do you think we'll get in trouble for trespassing?"

Nestor shook his head. "I don't see any signs posted and nobody's asking us to leave.

Besides, we're pursuing a suspect. That gives us a little leeway."

Following Mac, they made a beeline for the shed. Cora's tracks lead straight to the door and then disappeared. Nestor held up his hand without speaking, signaling James to stop. He drew his gun and crept toward the door. James stepped back and to the side, pulling the dog with him. Nestor crouched down next to the door, reached out with his free hand, and pushed the door open. Staying low, he swung around in front of the opening, gun first and swept the area inside. Finding no one, he stood up and holstered his weapon.

"Pump house." Nestor motioned at the wall opposite the door. "The whole backside is collapsed. She went straight through."

James stuck his head in the door and looked around. He saw a rusty pressure tank connected to a couple of pipes, and wires leading into a well casing. The wooden floor was cracked and broken in some places. Boards were missing in others. Something in the corner caught his attention.

"Hold on to Mac for a minute." James handed Nestor the leash. "I want to check something out."

Nestor held the dog back and watched as James made his way into the rickety structure. He knelt down, picked up a couple of splintered boards, and held them up to the light streaming in through a gap in the roof. Setting one of the chunks of wood off to the side, he fit the other one into a hole in the floor like a piece of a jigsaw puzzle, then held it up and turned back to Nestor.

"See the fresh break on this board? It's not weathered like the other ones." He pointed at the void in the floor. "And the ground's been disturbed under here."

Nestor lashed Mac's leash to a post and stepped inside. He crouched down and inspected the hole.

"She dug something with square corners out of there — like some kind of box."

"So, Mrs. Lewis hid something in this building." James stood up and brushed the dirt off of his knees. "I wonder what it was?"

"I don't know, but it had to be something important," Nestor replied. "Cora could have made a clean getaway, but she chose to come back up here to retrieve whatever was under those floorboards."

"Do you think it was money?"

Nestor shook his head. "I doubt it. If it was cash, she would have come back for it years ago."

"Maybe she was hiding some kind of evidence."

"Only one way to find out." Nestor stepped outside, untied the dog, and handed James the leash. "Let's get moving."

James and Mac took the lead again. They circled around to the back of the pump house and picked up Cora's trail near the collapsed wall. The footprints led down a rutted and overgrown dirt road before turning back toward the lower end of the ridge. Mac stayed locked onto Cora's scent as the terrain pitched up again. This time James was able to keep his footing and held a strong, steady pace until they reached the top. As they crested the ridge, James' phone came alive again. Before he could get the device out of his pocket, a shrill whistle rose from the direction of the cabin. Mac stopped short and let out a bark. Nestor turned his head in the direction of the sound.

"That's Emery's signal." He stepped around James and the dog. Breaking into a trot, he called back over his shoulder. "Now we need to run."

James struggled to keep his grip as Mac jerked on the leash and took off. The dog kept pace with Nestor, staying just off the man's heels. James was surprised that he had to work so hard to keep up with a man almost twice his age and at least 50 pounds heavier. Josh couldn't resist the opportunity to give his creator a little ribbing.

What's wrong, kid? Having trouble hangin' with the old man?

"That 'old man' has been chasing suspects longer than I've been alive," James replied in his head.

You need to get away from that damn computer – maybe hit the gym once in a while.

"I'll be taking a lot more walks now that I have a dog, but that isn't going to help me right now."

Nope. You're just gonna have to grit your teeth and push through it. Oh and we've got a book signing coming up next week. Try not to fall on our face.

Chapter 34

James tried to keep his feet under him as he and Nestor ran full speed down the steep hill. He struggled to stay upright every time his foot landed on a rock or a loose patch of soil. Mac surged a couple of times and pulled hard at the leash, tipping James off balance. He held his breath and extended his free arm like a tightrope walker to keep from falling over.

When they reached the bottom of the hill, Nestor hurdled the sagging barbed wire fence, never breaking his pace. Mac also cleared it with ease. James let go of the leash, stutter-stepped, and then sprang as high as he could. He tucked his feet, clearing the top wire by the narrowest of margins. Upon landing, his legs slid in opposite directions, sending him into a near panic. He quickly recovered by pushing off of a tree with one hand.

The trio burst out of the forest, sprinted around the side of the cabin and ran toward the garage. When they rounded the corner, James spied Emery sitting on the ground, his back against the garage wall. Mac ran straight to him, climbed in his lap and started licking his face. James grabbed the leash and pulled the dog off. Emery cursed under his breath and rubbed the back of his head.

"Damn fool woman," he grumbled. "Come up from behind and hit me with a big-ass rock."

Nestor pulled Emery's hat off and dug through the stringy hair on the back of his head.

"No blood, but you've got a pretty big knot coming up." He handed the hat back to Emery. "She knock you out?"

"No, but I've been seein' stars for couple minutes." He pulled the cap back over his gray mop and bobbled as he tried to stand.

Nestor reached down. "Need a hand?"

"I got it." Emery braced a shoulder against the wall, pushed off, and struggled to his feet. He headed for Nestor's truck, bobbing and weaving as he walked. "We gotta get a move on. She took off in Tally's car—got about a three or four minute head start on us."

"She can't outrun the radio." Nestor grabbed Emery by the upper arm and steadied him. "There's only a couple of roads out of here and we know what she's driving. I'll call it in once we're out of this valley."

James opened the back door of the truck and pointed inside. Mac jumped in and gave an excited yip as he waited for his master to climb in next to him. Nestor snapped his fingers to get James' attention and pointed to the other side of the truck as he guided Emery toward the open door.

"I want you in the front seat this time, Stray Dog. I need your eyes."

"Yeah, mine ain't focusing too good," Emery grunted, as he climbed in to the back seat. "Got my bell rung pretty hard."

"Probably didn't do the rock much good either." Nestor grinned and climbed into the driver's seat.

James got in and closed his door. He turned around to check on the dog before buckling his seatbelt. Mac settled in and laid his head on Emery's leg. Without looking down, Emery rested his hand on the dog's head and began stroking his soft fur like it was a natural reaction. He continued to rub the back of his own head with the other hand.

"Did Cora have anything with her?" James asked, still breathing heavy from the run.

Emery shrugged. "Looked like she threw an old tackle box or something in the car. Couldn't really see much with my face in the dirt and my marbles shook loose."

"That has to be what she came back for." James pointed over the hill. "She hid something in an old pump house in the next valley. Do you have any idea what it might be?"

Emery shook his head and winced in pain.

"No clue."

"When was the last time the two of you were out here?" Nestor asked, as he turned the truck around and headed down the hill.

"Been a long time—maybe ten years or more."

James scanned the road ahead. "I can't imagine what she could have left out here for over ten years that was important enough to come back for and risk getting caught."

"I doubt she even considered getting caught," Nestor replied. "She's in a different car and this place is way off the beaten path."

"You're probably right," James sighed. "She felt comfortable enough to stay at the cabin and start a fire."

Nestor gave a nod. "Maybe spent the night as well."

"Do you think she left anything inside that could help us?" James asked. "If she wasn't expecting anyone, she probably didn't have time to go back in and get her things."

"We'll have to get a search warrant to go in," Nestor replied. "But we'll worry about that later. Right now we need to focus on catching Cora."

James' eyes locked on the intersection with the main road as the truck emerged from between the ridges. He pointed at the ground in front of the truck.

"She went south. There are fresh tire marks over the ones me made coming in."

"Good eyes," Nestor responded, rounding the corner and driving the gas pedal just short of the floor. "Keep them open. We don't know how far ahead she is."

James grabbed Nestor's binoculars out of the glove compartment and focused on the horizon. "I wish the roads were drier. Her car isn't kicking up any dust that I can see."

"That's okay. There's only one way she can get out to the highway going this direction, and it's fifteen miles of dirt road to get there. No way she could have made it that far already." Nestor picked up his radio and called in the information on the car and driver. "If we don't catch up before we hit blacktop, they'll stop her on the other end."

James' phone pinged several times, alerting him to incoming messages. He lowered the binoculars and pulled his phone out of his pocket.

"It looks like we have cell service again." The phone rang, startling him. He dropped it in his lap, then scooped it up and looked at the screen. "It's Will. Maybe he got the information on the property."

Nestor nodded toward the ringing device.

"Are you going to answer it?"

"Oh . . ." James swiped the screen and put the phone up to his ear. "Hello?"

"Jimmy?" Will's voice shot from the phone loud enough for Nestor and Emery to hear. "Jimmy, where the hell have you been?"

"We were up in a canyon. We couldn't get a signal."

"Have you checked your text messages?"

"Not yet."

"You guys need to be careful," Will shouted. "That house belongs to —"

The phone cut off as the road dipped down into a wash.

"Will?" James pressed the phone hard against his ear. "Will? Are you still there?" He lowered the phone and slapped the dash in frustration. "Lost the signal again!"

"Check you messages, like he said," Nestor replied, as he slid the truck around a sweeping turn and back up out of a wash.

James gripped the door-handle with one hand and his phone in the other. He did his best to hold the phone steady as he poked at the screen with his thumb. When the messaging app finally opened, James hit Will's name and silently read the string of messages. Nestor straightened the truck out and glanced over at James.

"Well? Did he find out who owns that cabin?"

"Yeah, he got the information all right."

"Forward it to Alexander," Nestor instructed. "Fill him in on the situation and tell him I said to get a search warrant started."

"Um . . ." James chewed his lower lip as he looked up at Nestor. "There might be a problem with that."

"What's wrong?" Nestor slowed the truck down and locked eyes with James.

"The property owner." James held his phone up. "It's Martin Boles."

"Boles?" Nestor frowned and gritted his teeth. "I knew I'd been out there before. He picked that property up in a bank auction after he served papers to the previous owner."

"The damn County Sheriff—can you believe that, boy?" Emery looked down at Mac and rubbed the dog's head. "Hell, if I'd have known Cora had them kind of connections it might've saved me a night or two in the pokey."

"Wouldn't have done you any good," Nestor replied. "He wasn't the sheriff until he got elected a few years ago."

"Oh, well." Emery grinned. "Cora probably would've left me swinging in the breeze anyway."

James held up his phone. "There's another

message from Will. When he couldn't get a hold of us, he started driving up here."

"Did he say where he is?" Nestor asked.

"He sent the message when he stopped for gas at Cordes Junction. That was about fifteen minutes ago."

"When you get a signal, call him," Nestor instructed. "Give him the description of the car and tell him to hold up at the intersection of Route 69 and 169. If she gets past the units waiting where the road comes out in Dewey, then she has to go by him."

James checked his phone. Seeing it had a signal again, he dialed Will and put it on speaker this time. It only took one ring for Will to answer.

"Jimmy?" Will's voice sounded like he was in a wind tunnel. "We got cut off. Did you hear what I said? Sheriff Boles owns that house!"

"I saw your message," James replied. "Where are you?"

"Almost to Dewey. Where are you guys?"

"We're headed south on the main dirt road that goes by the property. We're trying to catch up with Cora Lewis," James replied. "Nestor wants you to watch the highway intersection in case she gets past the other officers. She's driving a blue —"

Will cut him off. "I heard the APB on my scanner. Listen, there's another way outta there. If it hasn't been washed out, she could cut back to the east instead and come out on 169 west of Dewey. That would keep her off 69 completely."

"Do you know where that road comes out?" Nestor asked.

"Yup, I've hunted up in that area before."

"Then head out there and come in from the other direction." Nestor accelerated the truck again. "We'll keep going toward Dewey until we catch up to her."

"Ten-four."

Chapter 35

Will made a hard right turn on Route 169, down shifted, and gunned his Jeep. He sped up the hill, around a sweeping turn, and then caught high gear. When he came up behind a slower vehicle, he hit the brakes, then swung out into the oncoming traffic lane and mashed the throttle as the road straightened out again. Will dove back into his lane in time to miss a pickup coming from the opposite direction. When he reached the spot where a set of power-line towers shadowed the road like giant skeletons, he jammed the brakes, cranked the steering wheel to the left, and hit the gas again, drifting the Jeep onto a dirt road. About a mile up the road he came to a Y and slowed down. He turned on the less traveled fork that veered back to the east.

"No way she's made it this far yet," he said to himself, pulling to the side. He opened the canvas door of the Jeep and leaned out to inspect the surface of the dirt road. "No fresh tracks."

Will grabbed his phone out of his pocket and typed a message to James.

WILL: On the power line road. No fresh tracks coming out this way.

JAMES: Nestor says to keep coming toward

us.

WILL: Got it. My road comes out where the power lines cross the one you're on.

JAMES: We'll watch for you.

Will put his phone away and started driving again, guiding the Jeep down the unmaintained road. Climbing up hills and down through washes, the road weaved its way back and forth between the high voltage line towers. Whenever Will slowed to an idle, he could hear the thick wires over his head crackle with electricity in the cold, dry air. The sound made the hair on the back of his neck stand on end. Each time he crossed under them, he sped up and tried not to touch any exposed metal for fear of getting a nasty shock.

Reaching the top of a ridge, Will stopped next to the tower that stood at the highest point on the line. He grabbed a pair of binoculars out of the backpack behind the passenger seat and jumped out of the vehicle. Standing on the front bumper, he scanned the area to the northwest where the power lines leveled out on the flat, grassy plain before turning north and disappearing behind the mountains. Crossing under the lines in the distance, he could barely make out what he assumed was the road James and Nestor were traveling. He hopped back in the Jeep, stowed the binoculars, and headed down into the next wash.

The farther Will went, the rougher the road became. The monsoon rains of the previous summer had cut through the small valleys, digging away the road in some places and depositing thick sandbars in others. At times he had to engage the Jeep's four-wheel-drive to make it through the rocky bottom of a dry wash before picking up the track on the other side.

"No way she made it through here in that low-slung car," he muttered gunning the engine and bouncing up an embankment. "I'll be damn lucky if *I* don't get stuck."

Will made his way over the ridge and dropped into the next depression. Before turning into the sandy wash at the bottom, he stopped the Jeep and looked upstream. As he scanned the other bank for where the road picked up, something caught his eye. He saw a patch of blue paint peeking through a gap in the trees and bushes, and the glint of sunlight off chrome.

"Jackpot." He eased the Jeep into the wash and crept slowly to the other side. "That's the same color as the car from the APB."

As he made his way up the embankment and back onto the road, Will unzipped his coat and reached inside. He placed his hand on the butt of the gun in his shoulder holster and flipped the safety off. Leaving the gun in place, he pulled his hand out and put it back on the wheel. Moving slowly, he kept an eye on the spot where he'd seen the patch of color.

The road curved around a stand of trees, then straightened about twenty yards from the blue sedan. One corner of the car sat lower than the others and Will could see someone in boots, jeans and a heavy jacket digging in the trunk. A jack and a tire-iron flew out and hit the ground. As he came to a stop, the person stood up, pulled the spare tire out and tossed it on the ground next to the other items. It was a woman—a gray haired, hard looking woman.

"Matches the description," Will mumbled under his breath.

He couldn't hear the woman's voice over the growl of the Jeep's engine, but he didn't need to. You didn't have to be an expert lip reader to recognize the string of expletives she let fly as he pulled up in front of the car..

"And she's got anger issues." He slipped his phone out to send James a message, but there was no signal. "No phone means no backup. Better play this one cool."

Will shut the Jeep off and stepped out. He gave a friendly wave as he cautiously approached the irate woman. "Need a hand?"

Cora Lewis came around the car and kicked at the right front wheel. "Blew a damn tire."

"You keep heading this direction and you'll have more than a tire to deal with," Will reached down and picked up the jack. "I'll help you get rolling, but you're gonna have to go back out the way you came. The road's washed out in half a dozen places between here and the highway."

"Can't go back," Cora replied with a sneer. "Road's blocked that way too."

"Really?" Will crouched down, pushed the jack under the car, and grabbed the lug wrench. "If the road's blocked, how'd you get this far?"

Cora hesitated. "Um . . . rock slide — happened behind me after I came through."

"Well, you're just having a hell of a day." Will kept his face down so she couldn't see him smile. "But it looks like your luck is changing. I've got a winch and couple of shovels in the Jeep. Maybe we can clear the road enough for you get by."

"No!" Cora stepped back and looked over her shoulder. "Ah . . . it's a boulder — big boulder — can't move it."

"Maybe we can call for help." Will pointed at the phone sticking out of her coat pocket. "Know anybody with a tractor?"

Cora stiffened up. "Can't call . . . no signal

here."

"I'm sure we can figure something out." Will could see Cora fidgeting and pacing like a trapped animal. He fumbled with the wrench while he thought about how to deescalate the situation. "How about we get this fixed, then we'll worry about how to get you out of here, okay?"

"Yeah." She stopped pacing and took a breath. "Yeah, let's just get it fixed."

Will kept one eye on Cora as she went to retrieve the spare tire. The way the cuff of her jeans moved when she walked caught his attention. As an undercover cop, it was a movement he knew all too well. The sharp protrusion moving back and forth on the side of her leg with every step told she had something stashed in the top of her boot— something like a knife or a gun. As she rolled the tire toward him, Will tried to come up with some way to stall while he considered his options. He reached under the car and moved the jack around, purposely banging it against the frame a few times to make some noise before pulling it out.

"Car's sitting too low to get the jack under." Will nodded his head toward the Jeep. "I've got a high-lift jack. I can pick it up with that."

"Whatever you gotta do, just do it," Cora snapped. "I need to get outta here."

Will went around to the back of his Jeep and

opened the canvas flap. Using the vehicle as cover, he slipped his phone out and typed a message to James. *Hope that makes it out,* he thought as he put the phone back and un-strapped the jack from the roll bar.

By the time Will made it back to the car, Cora's face was getting red, and despite the cool temperature he could see beads of sweat forming above her brow.

"How long is this gonna take? I really need to get moving."

"Shouldn't be long now," Will replied slipping the jack under the bumper of the car. "Once I get this off the ground we're in good shape with the car, but we still have to figure out how to get you out of here."

Cora eyed Will's Jeep and then the tire iron on ground in front of her.

"I got a few ideas . . ."

Chapter 36

Nestor accelerated the truck across the flat, grassy plain as James scanned the dirt road ahead with the binoculars.

"I really thought we'd be able to see her by now."

"So did I," Nestor replied. "We're not that far from Dewy and the units stationed there haven't been able to get eyes on her either."

James turned around to address Emery. "How well does your wife know this area?"

"Pretty damn well," Emery replied, gripping the door handle with one hand and the dog with the other. "Lived here all her life."

"Do you think she knows about the other road?"

Emery nodded. "She knows these hills inside and out—used to hunt out here with her dad and her brothers."

James turned back around and looked at the rolling grassland stretching out in front of them. The power line towers dominated the horizon, with the small town of Dewey in the distance.

"We're almost to the power line road turnoff." James pointed up the road. "We haven't seen any sign of her, so I think we should go that way."

"I agree." Nestor slowed the truck as they approached the towers. "If she keeps going straight they can pick her up at the highway. I doubt she'll try to double back and head north as long as she thinks we're still behind her."

Nestor passed under the power lines and turned onto the narrow track. It wasn't long before the road grew rougher and started gaining elevation. They passed under the lines and around a tower at the top of the hill before descending into a wash. A single set of fresh tire tracks cut through the sandy bottom, then up the other side. One track was relatively smooth, the other deep and broken up.

"Whoever came through here last had a little trouble with the sand," Nestor observed. "Narrow tires, two-wheel-drive and no traction."

"How do you know?" James asked.

"One tire was digging in and the other wasn't. If they had a limited slip differential or traction control, both tire tracks would be the same."

"And the narrow tires mean it was probably a car, rather than a truck or a Jeep?" James added.

"Exactly." Nestor smiled. "Which means the odds of that car getting stuck are pretty high, especially if this road gets any worse. She may end up catching herself."

"At the very least it's going to slow her down more than it does us." As they ascended the hill on the other side of the wash, James noticed several of the larger rocks that had fresh scrape marks on their surfaces. "It looks like the car is bottoming out. It has to be Mrs. Lewis, right? Anyone else would have turned around if their car was getting damaged."

"Yeah, she's a stubborn old goat," Emery spat. "And a damn fool sometimes."

"I'd say the odds of it being Cora are in our favor," Nestor replied. "We're on the right track."

When the truck broke over the top of the next hill, James caught sight of two vehicles below. He tapped Nestor on the arm.

"Hold up." He pointed down the hill between the trees. "I see the top of the car, and I think that's Will's Jeep in front of it."

Nestor inched the truck forward until he could see through the branches. "That's her. Looks like she blew a tire and Packrat's fixing it for her."

"Will's changing her tire?" James grabbed the binoculars again and focused in on his brother. "Why is he fixing her car? Do you think he doesn't know it's her?"

"He knows," Nestor replied with a quick nod. "But I'm guessing she has no idea he's a cop. He's doing what any good undercover officer does when he doesn't have backup—he's sizing up the situation before he acts. Fixing the tire gives him time to determine if she's armed or not, and the best way to proceed."

"He'd better figure it out fast," James replied, still looking through the binoculars. "She just picked up something off the ground." James gasped. "It's a tire iron!"

Nestor laid on the truck's horn and hit the gas. The truck roared to life, throwing gravel into the air as it lurched forward and slammed James back in his seat. They rounded the corner at the bottom of the hill just in time to see Cora drop the tire iron and run into the brush between the road and the wash. Will rubbed the back of his head as he struggled to his feet. He regained his composure and took off after her. Nestor sped past the car and the Jeep, running halfway off the road to get by. He turned into the wash and pointed the truck upstream, but had to stop before hitting a rock shelf.

Nestor and James both bailed out of the truck. Mac jumped over the front seat and out the open door, chasing after James. Nestor pointed up the hill on the opposite side of the wash.

"Head for the high ground," he shouted. "If you spot her, you can guide me in."

James followed Nestor's command. He cut

through the bushes on the edge of the wash and onto the road with Mac hot on his heels, still dragging his leash. When James reached the top of the ridge, he could see up the wash for about two hundred yards before it turned east and went behind another hill. In the bottom he saw Nestor quickly catching up to Will, who was stumbling and still holding the back of his head. Nestor slowed to check on him, but Will waved him on as he sat down on a large rock. James estimated that Cora had an eighty yard lead on the men—just enough to make it around the corner and up the bank while out of Nestor's line of sight. She ducked into the trees, but James was still able to track her by the flash of her orange jacket between the branches. He cupped his hands around his mouth and yelled to get Nestor's attention, then waved him in the direction she was headed. Nestor waved back and followed Cora's tracks out of the wash.

James headed off the road and continued up the spine of the ridge. He studied the terrain in front of him, trying to determine what route the fleeing woman would be most likely to take. He reasoned the sharp incline and rocky shelf to the north would force her to keep moving east and eventually lead her up to the same ridge he was on. He picked up speed, pacing himself to arrive first at the spot where he figured Cora would emerge. Reaching the area, he slowed down and looked for a place to hide. As Mac surged by him, James grabbed the leash.

"Hold on, boy." James yanked the leash and crouched behind a bush, pulling the dog close. "We've got to hide and be quiet, or we'll lose the element of surprise."

And then what? Josh echoed inside his brain. *She might have a weapon and all you've got is a pocketknife and a mangy dog.*

"You're right. I need a plan." James looked around to see what was within reach. He picked up the biggest rock he could grip with one hand. "This will have to do."

A rock? Josh grunted. *That's your plan? Throw rocks at her?*

"Do you have a better idea?"

Give me a minute and I'm sure I can come up with something better than that.

"We don't have a minute."

James could hear heavy breathing and the sound of the stiff brush scraping against the nylon of Cora's jacket as she pushed her way up the hill. When she emerged from the brush, Mac barked and ducked out from under James' arm.

Cora spun around. "What the hell?"

She backed up as the dog tugged at the leash, pulling James out from his hiding place. As soon as she saw his face, she bent down and pulled up the cuff of her jeans, exposing a small pistol stashed in the top of her right boot. Mac broke away and ran at Cora. She stood back up, pistol in hand, and pointed in the dog's direction. Fearing for his new companion's life, James cocked his arm back and hurled the rock with everything he had. The projectile smashed into the side of Cora's face, knocking her off balance and sending her to the ground as she let out an ear-piercing scream.

She tried to raise her gun hand again, but Mac landed in the middle of her body. He bit down on her arm just above the wrist. She screamed again and let the gun drop. Running to the dog's aid, James kicked the gun out of reach and grabbed Mac's collar.

"Down, boy!" He pulled back hard on the dog. "Let her go!"

Mac released his jaw as Nestor topped the hill and ran toward them. He knelt down next to Cora, pulled out his handcuffs, and slapped them around her wrists. He eyed the side of Cora's bloody face, then the softball sized rock laying on the ground a few feet away. Looking up at James, Nestor smiled and gave a nod of approval.

"Nice take-down, Stray Dog. Congratulations on your first collar."

Chapter 37

James sorted through the piles on the table of the sheriff's office conference room. He organized the loose stacks of paper and reports, filing them into the proper boxes, while Nestor erased the two large whiteboards on the opposite side of the room.

"I can't believe this is over," James sighed. "I actually feel a little sad about it. Is that weird?"

"Not at all." Nestor put the eraser down and turned to face James. "When something's consumed your every thought for this long, it leaves a void when it comes to an end. This case has been a part of my life for fourteen years, so I understand how you feel, but it's not quite over yet."

"The contents of the box Cora Lewis came back for, right?"

"Right." Nestor opened one of the folders on the table. "It's not going to be easy, but it has to be dealt with."

James half-smiled. "Is this one of those teaching moments where you want me to learn by handling it myself?"

"No, this needs to come from me." He thumbed through the papers in the folder. "Things might get a little rough. You're welcome to step out of the room if you want."

"I can't do that," James replied as he walked around the table and stood next to Nestor. "You've had my back through this whole experience — even trusted my instincts when I didn't. It's my turn to have your back."

Nestor grinned and placed his hand on James' shoulder. He opened his mouth to speak, but closed it immediately when the door to the conference room swung open. Sheriff Boles strutted in like he owned the place. His eyes shifted from side to side, surveying the entire room before settling on the two men standing across the table. His politician's smile was absent, replaced by a flat, expressionless poker-face. James noted this was the first time he'd seen the man enter the room without removing his cowboy hat.

"So, you finally got your man," he grunted in a sandpaper voice.

"Woman," Nester corrected with a face just as expressionless as the sheriff's. "Picked her up day before yesterday."

"Yeah, I got the memo." Boles waved several pieces of paper stapled together in the air. "I was served a search warrant for my cabin this morning. I've got to hand it to you, Yazzi. You've got some pretty big cojones."

"Just following procedure." Nestor crossed

his arms and straightened his back. "You had a murder suspect hiding there."

"She wasn't a suspect when she showed up," he huffed. "She said she needed a place to cool off for a couple of days. I figured it had something to do with that loser husband of hers."

"Doesn't matter," Nestor replied in a monotone. "She was staying there when she was caught, so we need to search for anything she may have left behind when she ran."

"This isn't right." Boles threw the warrant on the table and paced back and forth. "I know you're gunning for my job, Yazzi You want to be sheriff? Is that the deal?"

"I want to get to the truth. That's all I've ever wanted."

"Yeah, well the truth is you want me out of here." Boles stopped pacing and looked at James. "You and your little sidekick want to run this county? Be my guest."

Boles turned toward the door and took a step. Nestor picked up the folder off the table and held it up.

"Don't you want to know what we found?"

Boles stopped and spun around. "What are you talking about? Alexander just headed out there to tear my house apart."

"In the car," Nestor replied. "What we

found in the car she was driving. Cora was already out of town, but she came back for something—a box she had hidden."

The sheriff eyed the papers in Nestor's hand. "Is that the contents?"

"Copies—the originals are already logged into evidence and locked up."

Boles pulled out a chair and dropped into it. Nestor tossed the file down in front of him and stepped back. Boles opened the folder and scanned each page before slowly turning to the next. Reaching the last sheet, he closed the folder and lifted his gaze, locking eyes with Nestor.

"You should have come to me first when you found this."

"That wouldn't be proper procedure." Nestor reached across and pulled the folder back to his side of the table. "We wouldn't want to break the chain of evidence and put the case in jeopardy."

The sheriff's expression hardened. "Who else besides the two of you has seen this?"

"David and a few members of his team," Nestor replied. "And Stray Dog's brother—he's Phoenix PD."

"You got another jurisdiction involved in this?" Boles jumped to his feet, sending his chair rolling backward into the wall. "What the hell were you thinking? Who signed off on that?"

"He happened to be in the neighborhood when we were in pursuit." Nestor let a little smile escape. "When time is of the essence and someone you trust offers to help, you don't say no."

"We're gonna talk about this, Yazzi." Boles shook a finger at Nestor. "This one might cost you your badge."

Boles stormed out of the room and slammed the door hard enough that James was afraid it might fly off the hinges.

"Could you really lose your job?"

"For following procedure?" Nestor shook his head. "No. He could make something else up, but he won't. He's like a snake—he'll find some crack to slither through and get out of this."

James picked up the folder and opened it. Some of the pages contained pictures of the sheriff playing cards with several different people, including Cora Lewis. A few of the photos were of a more compromising nature, causing James to blush. Other pages were copies of IOUs, lists of times and places, and notes detailing favors Boles had done for people to clear some of his debts.

"I still don't understand why Cora came back for this." James sat on the edge of the table. "It's not likely Sheriff Boles could have got a murder charge against her dropped, even if she threatened to expose these things."

"She was dead broke. My guess is she was just pressing him for enough money to get as far from here as she could."

"And she just happened to have evidence against the county sheriff?" James shook his head. "She had to have some other plan when she collected this information."

Nestor smiled. "You're thinking like a cop again—keep going. I want to see where you take this."

James thumbed through a couple more pages. "Everything is dated after Virgil disappeared."

Nestor nodded. "I noticed that too."

"My guess is she met Sheriff Boles at a poker game some time after she killed Virgil and saw an opportunity to gain some leverage, so she started collecting." James put the folder down. "That box was her insurance policy if Virgil's body was ever found."

"Sounds reasonable. Go on"

"When we located the body, she probably panicked," James continued. "I'll bet if we check her cell phone we'll find calls between Cora and Sheriff Boles."

"You think she tried to get him to influence the investigation?" Nestor asked.

"Well, he did pressure you to arrest Emery Lewis for the murder before we even got into the new evidence," James replied.

"So you think Cora tried to get him to throw Emery under the bus?"

"Judging by the way she talked about him the day we spoke to her out at her trailer, I wouldn't doubt it. She could have accomplished two goals at the same time—pinning the murder on someone else and getting rid of her alcoholic husband."

"I like your theory, but I doubt Cora will confirm it when we question her." Nestor patted James on the back. "Come on, we've still got some work to do, then we'll get this case packed up and over to the D.A's office" Nestor paused. "And then I'd like your help with one more thing."

Chapter 38

James stared out the window as Nestor piloted the truck down the winding dirt road past small farms now fallow for the winter. He watched, mouth agape, as the colorful landscape rolled by. Tall cliffs of red, brown, purple, and gray rose majestically on their right, while tan and pink sands covered the flatter ground to the left. James rolled his window down and let the cold, December air bite at his skin.

"It so beautiful," he said with the wonder of a child seeing Christmas lights for the first time. "I thought it would be desolate and depressing out here, but it's amazing. It looks like someone painted the landscape."

"A lot of people have that picture in their minds when you talk about the Navajo Nation," Nestor replied. "They have no idea what lays within our borders. I've been around the world and seen many wonders, but for me, none match the beauty of my homeland."

"This is the farthest I've ever been from my home." James popped his collar up and pulled it tight around his neck. "I'd love to travel now that . . . you know."

"Now that your mother has passed?"

"Yeah." James lowered his head. "I don't

mean her any disrespect, but she hid the whole world from me. I've never climbed a mountain or seen the ocean—it hasn't even been a year since I touched snow for the first time. I want to go places—see the things I've only written about."

"Be patient, Stray Dog." Nestor had a thin smile as he glanced over at the young man in his passenger seat. "You've come a long way in a year. I've seen some big changes even in the short time I've known you."

"Things really are different now. I have a girlfriend and a real family." James rolled the window back up and looked at Nestor. "I also have a mentor. If someone told me a year ago I'd be investigating a murder, I would have thought they were crazy."

"None of us know what we'll be doing in a year, Stray Dog. There were times I thought this day would never come, but it has."

"What is this day?" James asked. "You still haven't told me why you wanted to bring me out here."

"This is where Virgil and I grew up." Nestor turned the truck up a rutted side road and stopped at the end. "Welcome to Moenave Canyon—my home."

Nestor opened his door and reached into the backseat to retrieve a leather bag before stepping out. He slung the long strap attached to the bag over his shoulder and stood in front of the truck. James got out and joined him.

"I take it we're here because of Virgil." James eyed the bag on Nestor's shoulder. "Are his ashes in there?"

Nestor shook his head. "No, it's something else. I'll explain when we get to the top."

James tucked his hands in the pockets of his coat and stared up at the high walls of the narrow canyon. "We have to climb up there?"

"There's a trail just around the corner." Nestor pointed with his lower lip. "I'm too old to get up there the way Virgil and I used to do it."

Nestor led the way up the narrow trail and around a bend. The farther they ventured into the canyon, the closer the colorful walls came together. The hike reminded James of the day he met Nestor for the first time. They were brought together in the foothills of the Bradshaw Mountains by another murder and ended up trekking into a similar landscape. It was also the day he was tagged with the name Stray Dog, a label he'd come not only to tolerate, but to embrace.

Near the head of the canyon, they began ascending the wall on what appeared to be a trail worn into the earth by livestock. Nestor was as sure-footed as ever, as James slipped here and there. When they reached the top, Nestor paused and looked back down at the valley below. A smile crossed his lips as he took in a deep breath and let it out slowly.

"I've missed this place," he said, almost too soft for James to hear. "I shouldn't have waited so long to come back."

"Why did you leave?" James asked, between heavy breaths. "Did something happen?"

Nestor nodded. "Life happened. Virgil and I enlisted right after graduation. After seeing so much of the world, this place felt too small — too isolated." He turned back toward James. "I was young, wild, and didn't know what I had here. By the time I learned to appreciate it, I was already established somewhere else."

"It feels peaceful here," James replied, looking over the fields and houses below. "This is the total opposite of where I live. I'm right in the middle of the city. It's never this quiet, even in the middle of the night."

"Prescott is a nice compromise — big enough to have everything thing you need, but still a small-town feel." Nestor turned away from the edge of the canyon and pointed to the east. "Let's get back to it. We're almost there."

They walked another two hundred yards and then cut back toward the edge of the cliff.

Nestor stopped next to a small mound about twenty feet from the edge. He knelt and uprooted a clump of grass. He used the bundle to sweep away the sand that had blown up against the mound, revealing a pile of rocks, some as small as a coin, others up to softball size. The rocks varied in color, shape and composition. Most of them looked nothing like the stones covering the ground in the surrounding area.

James knelt on the other side of the mound. "What's this?"

"A rock pile."

James smiled and rolled his eyes. "I can see that, but is there another name your people use for it?"

"Not that you can pronounce." Nestor looked up and grinned. "In English, it literally translates to 'rock pile.'"

"What's the significance of it? These rocks don't look like they came from around here."

"Good eye, Stray Dog." Nestor picked up a round, black stone and wiped it off. Its surface looked to have been polished by years in the water. "This one is from Okinawa. I picked it up on the same beach where my grandfather landed in World War II." Next, he held up a rough piece of weathered granite. "This came from Afghanistan, where Virgil and I served."

"So, it's a place to deposit reminders of your past?"

"No, it's much more." Nestor sat down on the cold ground and crossed his legs. "Let me explain."

James sat opposite Nestor, pulled up another clump of grass, and began helping to sweep debris from the mound. Nestor cleared his throat and began his tale.

"Below these cliffs, we used to sit around the fire in the evening and listen to my grandfather tell stories. He told us of his childhood, his time as a Code Talker, and spoke of the old ways. This is the way our people have traditionally passed on our history to the next generation. One night he told us of the rock piles. In the old days, every clan had a place that held special meaning for them. This would be the place they would make their pile."

"What's the significance of the rocks?" James asked. "Do they have a special meaning, or are they like a territory marker?"

"Each rock has a special meaning," Nestor replied. "During their daily routines or travels, sometimes a rock would catch their attention. It might be the color or the shape that made it stand out, or it simply spoke to them in some manner. Sometimes they would seek out a special rock for a specific purpose."

"But you still haven't told me what that purpose is." James shifted his weight to get blood flow back into one of his legs. "Why did they bring them home and put them on the pile?"

"You sound like me and Virgil when we were young." Nestor smiled and brushed the soil from a few more rocks. "Be patient and listen. You'll have your answer soon enough."

"Sorry." James went back to cleaning the pile as well.

Nestor continued. "At special times, the clan members would bring a rock, place it on the pile, and make a promise. The rock represented that promise — a commitment to someone. It might be a promise to watch over the family or a sick friend. Maybe a friend or relative was going through a hard time. The rock signified that commitment to support and be with them, in both this world and the next — now and forever."

Nestor placed the black beach stone back on the pile. "This one is for my grandfather, to thank him for all he taught me, and to promise we would be together again."

"Amazing." James choked back the lump of emotion in his throat. "I never imagined a little pile of rocks could hold so much meaning."

"Some of the piles were used for

generations. They might be three or four feet high." Nestor lowered his head. "But you don't see these piles much anymore. The practice has fallen by the wayside and most have been covered by the sands of time. Virgil and I started this one after we heard the story. It was our way of promising to keep the old ways alive and to always be there for each other and the ones we love."

"So, each one of these rocks is a promise you or Virgil made?"

"Every one of them. The last time I placed a stone here, I promised Virgil I would find him and bring him home. That was fourteen years ago." Nestor reached into the leather bag and produced a rugged, grayish-black volcanic rock shaped like a fist. "This came from the site where his body was recovered. It represents the promise kept, and a commitment to meet again in the next world." He held the rock out in front of James. "You found him, Stray Dog. You deserve the honor of placing the stone."

James reached out and cupped his hands. Nestor gently laid the rock in the bowl formed by his palms.

"Are you sure you want me to do this? He was your best friend — almost a brother."

"Not almost," Nestor replied as his eyes began to well up. "He was a brother in every way that mattered. If it weren't for you, we may never have found him. He would approve of you doing this."

"What do I say?"

"Whatever your heart tells you."

James cradled the special stone in his hands, and then gently placed it at the apex of the mound. "This is for you, Virgil. I've learned so much about you over the last few weeks. If you were still here, I think we would have been friends. I look forward to meeting you in the next world."

"That was perfect." A single tear rolled down Nestor's cheek. "It sounds like you're starting to figure out what you believe."

James sniffed and let a few tears escape as well. "I guess maybe I am. What I *can't* believe is that all of this is random—that life is one big cosmic accident. Too many things had to fall into just the right place."

"You're on a good path, Stray Dog." Nestor pulled out a bandana and handed it to James. "You keep heading in this direction and you'll make a fine godfather to that child."

"Thank you for being my guild on that path," James replied. "I never could made it this far without you."

Nestor smiled and bowed his head. "I think we made a pretty fair trade."

James stood up and wiped the tears from his face. He turned into the breeze and felt the cool wind dry the last moisture from his cheeks.

"This place *is* special. I've never been here before, and yet it feels like home." He turned to face his mentor. "Missy said something to me once—that I never really had a father figure. She said I was looking to you to fill that role. I think she was right."

"She's a smart girl. I would be honored to have a son like you." He rose and stood next to James. "My daughter might object to picking up a brother, but she'll get used to the idea."

James managed a little smile, but quickly became solemn once more.

"Would it be okay if I added a stone to your pile?"

"I don't see why not. You're as good as family now."

James reached into his pocket and pulled his hand back out. He unclenched his fist and held out his hand. In the palm was the round, flat stone Nestor had given him as a reminder of a lesson he had learned the hard way.

"I've carried this with me every day since you gave it to me. I think it qualifies as a special stone."

"Very special," Nestor replied. "It

represents a bond between us that can never be broken — not in this world or the next."

"This is my promise to my new families, both the Dugans and the Yazzis." James smiled at Nestor, bent down, and placed the stone on the pile. "I will always do my best to support all of you, as you've supported me. May we always be together, in this world and the next."

Nestor picked the leather bag up off the ground and put an arm around James's shoulders.

"Come on, Stray Dog. Let's go introduce you to the rest of the family."

Thank you for reading *Cold Karma*. If you enjoyed it, please take a moment to leave a review where you purchased the novel, and look for the first James McCarthy adventures, Killing Karma and Catching Karma.

About the Author

Eldred Bird is an Arizona based writer of contemporary fiction. Using the Phoenix metropolitan area as a home base, his stories reflect the broad diversity of scenery and humanity found within The Grand Canyon State.

For information on upcoming books and projects, follow him on the web at http://eldredbird.com.

Facebook:
https://www.facebook.com/EldredBirdAuthor/

Twitter and Instagram:
@EldredBird

Acknowledgements

I would like to thank the following people, without whom this book could never have been completed.

Debi Bird – Chief Editor, Graphic Designer, and Understanding Wife

Ed & Joanne Robinson – Content and Line Editors

Martin Fischer – Proofreader

The West Valley Writer's Critique Group of Avondale, Arizona – A special group of writers who took the time listen to me read every chapter out loud, and then told me what I *needed* to hear, not what I *wanted* to hear.